BROTHER IN ICE

Conquest of a Tabular Iceberg

After the Shipwreck

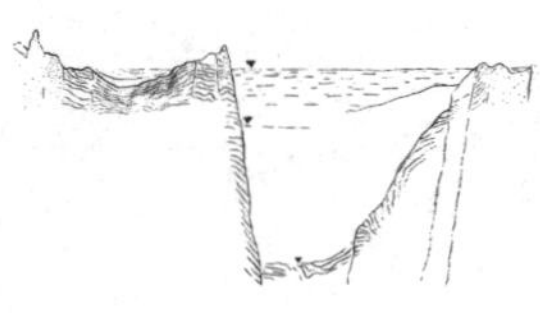

Conquest of Loss

Conquest of a ~~Room~~ House of One's Own

Conquest of Stability

Not Having to Be Realistic

Climbing first, rolling after

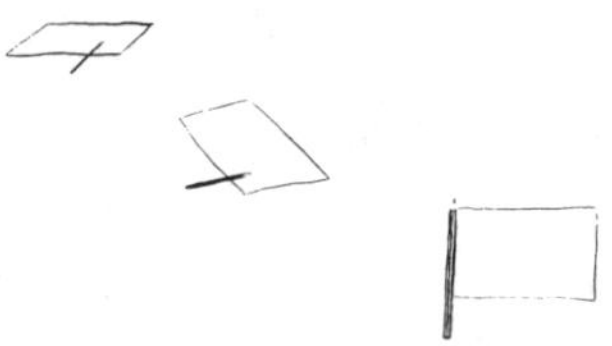

Sufficient Internal Resources in a Hostile Environment

A Simple Life

An Ordinary Life

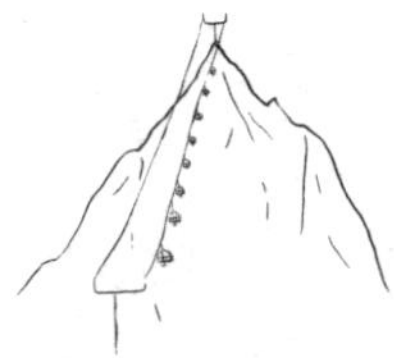

A Privileged Life

The Fake Peak

More, More, More

Conquest Overbooking

BROTHER IN ICE

Alicia Kopf

Translated by
Mara Faye Lethem

SHEFFIELD – LONDON – NEW HAVEN

First published in English translation by And Other Stories in 2018
Sheffield – London – New Haven
www.andotherstories.org

First published as *Germà de gel* in 2015 by L'Altra editorial, Barcelona.

This edition is published by arrangement with L'Altra Editorial c/o MB Agencia Literaria S.L. through Corinne Chabert Literary Agency.

9 8 7 6 5 4 3 2 1

This book is a work of fiction. Any resemblance to actual persons, living or dead, events or places is entirely coincidental.

ISBN: 978-1-911508-20-5
eBook ISBN: 978-1-911508-21-2

Editor: Stefan Tobler; Proofreader: Gesche Ipsen; Typesetter: Tetragon, London; Typefaces: Linotype Neue Swift and Verlag; Cover Design: Pablo Marfá; Line-drawing artworks: Alicia Kopf. Printed and bound by the CPI Group (UK) Ltd, Croydon CR0 4YY.

A catalogue record for this book is available from the British Library.

This book has been selected to receive financial assistance from English PEN's "PEN Translates" programme, supported by Arts Council England. English PEN exists to promote literature and our understanding of it, to uphold writers' freedoms around the world, to campaign against the persecution and imprisonment of writers for stating their views, and to promote the friendly co-operation of writers and the free exchange of ideas. www.englishpen.org

This book was also supported using public funding by Arts Council England.

CONTENTS

I. FROZEN HEROES

II. LIBRARY ATOP AN ICEBERG

To my brother, who isn't of ice

I want to be there, looking out, instead of out here looking in.

LOUISE BOYD, ARCTIC EXPLORER

It's an ambition of mine, which I never seem to get around to realizing, to spend at least one winter north of the Arctic Circle. Anyone can go there in the summer when the sun is up, but I want to go there when the sun is down, I really do, and so help me I'm going to do it one of these times.

GLENN GOULD

After the martyrs of the faith, those of science are the most admirable, and among them, the most heroic are the sailors of the polar seas . . . In the history of journeys there are no more curious episodes, no more impressive images, no more event-filled dramas than those of the winters in the ice-fields.

JULES VERNE

It wasn't until 1930 that the American chemist and bookseller William Barrow discovered that, to keep paper from degrading and yellowing, it had to be treated with a base coat during the production process (of calcium or magnesium bicarbonate) to neutralize the acids found in wood pulp, and prevent the formation of additional acids.

LORENZO DÁVALOS

What was silent in the father speaks in the son, and often I found in the son the unveiled secret of the father.

FRIEDRICH NIETZSCHE, *THUS SPOKE ZARATHUSTRA*

Men wanted for hazardous journey, small wages, bitter cold, long months of complete darkness, constant danger, safe return doubtful, honour and recognition in case of success.

ERNEST SHACKLETON (ATTRIBUTED)

Buenas noches, señores y señoras. La primera pregunta es . . . Qué es más macho, iceberg or volcano?

LAURIE ANDERSON, *DRUM DANCE & SMOKE RINGS*

. . . snow comes in through my shoes when Luis María dances with me and his hand on my waist rises in me like midday heat, like a tang of pungent oranges, of thrashed cane, and they hit her and it's impossible to resist and then I have to tell Luis María that I'm not well, that it's the dampness, dampness in the snow I don't feel, that I can't feel and that is coming in through my shoes.

JULIO CORTÁZAR, FROM "THE DISTANCES"

There is no more a method for learning than a method for finding treasures.

GILLES DELEUZE, *DIFFERENCE AND REPETITION*

Inveniam viam aut faciam (I shall find a way or make one)

SENECA

I

FROZEN HEROES

POLES

First it was the tabular icebergs, which appeared floating in the local pool. Narwhals got in through a crack in the tiles at the bottom. In the chlorinated water, I squeezed a bit of white ice in my hand, making a game of sinking it and letting it resurface. A dream. Later, at the Musée d'Orsay in Paris, I saw icecaps in the blue tutus of Degas's ballerinas.

I began to study. I learned that "arctic" comes from the Greek word *árktikos*, "near the bear," and "Antarctic," from *antárktikos*, "the place with no bears," but rather penguins. I learned that compasses are useless at the poles, rotational axes with shifting magnetic fields; north, the quintessential cardinal point, is actually not even an entirely stationary point of reference. At the poles even the ground moves. The early-twentieth-century polar explorers were mystics in search of the Holy Grail. Joseph Conrad said that their aims were as pure as the air at the high latitudes they surveyed. But those explorers were more like regular folks than we think – setting aside the fact that they risked their lives for a mission – because, as their journals show, they were also envious, and made mistakes, and told lies. Many explorers died trying to get to regions others erroneously claimed to have reached. The controversy over who discovered the North Pole is a fascinating chapter in polar history; more than just improbable feats taking place at a vague location, it is the story of one man's word against another's.

I am also searching for something in my white, unheated iceberg studio. An imaginary point that is completely unknown – and therefore absolutely magnetic. Sometimes I lose my way; I'm-cold-it's-late-still-waiting-on-a-paycheck.

a) I return home.

b) I return to the anchorage point, the word *pols* (poles) and its range of literal meanings in Catalan:

> *pols, el*, n. masc: the steadiness of hand needed to carry out certain acts, such as writing or holding a weapon.

And then, when you swap the masculine article for the feminine one, you arrive at more meanings of the word, which veer off in an unlikely direction yet could possibly link to my research:

> *pols, la*, n. fem: fine, dry powder consisting of tiny particles of earth or waste matter lying on the ground or on surfaces or carried in the air. Also, a type of snow: powder snow.

SYMZONIA

In the first few decades of the nineteenth century, Captain John Cleves Symmes defended the theory that the Earth had two holes – one at either end – that went right through it. Like *matryoshka* dolls, he claimed, the Earth housed the entrance to seven worlds that were nestled inside each other. Enough sunlight came in through the holes to sustain some sort of life, something that the captain aspired to demonstrate with complicated calculations and diagrams. If man could reach the pole, he would have an entire inner universe within reach.

This theory was a very fertile one for literature; from *Symzonia*, a novel by Symmes that recreates an underground world, to *The Narrative of Arthur Gordon Pym of Nantucket* by Edgar Allan Poe. Those works inspired *An Antarctic Mystery* and *Journey to the Center of the Earth* by Jules Verne. Many people believed that seas of ice at the poles led to Symmes's inner worlds, until the poles were finally conquered.

It was Sir John Barrow, in the nineteenth century, who awakened interest in the Arctic when he went in search of Sir John Franklin and the members of his expedition, who had disappeared trying to find the Northwest Passage. Following his example, the more ambitious nations embarked on various expeditions to conquer the two most extreme points of the Earth, hidden behind the mystique of storms and ice.

According to polar historian Fergus Fleming, the Arctic furor reached such heights that it was the subject of jokes in Europe and the United States. Was there a pole at the Pole? Was it made of wood? Did it have stripes like a barber's pole? The Inuit called it the "Great Nail."

The fact that the conquest of the North Pole entailed a group of individuals confronting the elements was incomprehensible to many. The strategic, economic, and scientific justifications were vague. Great Britain was hesitant, while other world powers had already decided that reaching the poles was a question of national glory.

> If only the moral advantage derived from these expeditions be considered, I believe that it would suffice to compensate for the sacrifices they demand. As men who surmount difficulties in their daily struggles feel themselves strengthened for encounters with yet greater difficulties, so should also a nation feel itself encouraged and stimulated by the success won by its sons to persevere in striving for greatness and prosperity.

These words were written by the Italian aristocrat Luigi Amedeo Giuseppe Maria Ferdinando Francesco di Savoia-Aosta, Duke of the Abruzzi, leader of the first Italian expedition to the North Pole.

MATRYOSHKA
OR THE HOLLOW NARRATOR THEORY

As in Symmes's theory, the narrative voice of this novel takes the form of seven different figures. The first one heads toward the city center dressed in black. She is so young that her features are fuzzy:

If you actually walk on a moving walkway, you go twice as fast. Some hundred meters ahead of myself, I proceed along the walkway, turn the corner without rotating my body and arrive at the store. I leave my bag in the closet and stand behind the counter. My hologram always arrives punctually. It's a shame the supervisor doesn't notice.

One right turn and a hundred meters further back, my physical self rushes to make it in on time. Once there, after straightening the piles of pullovers and reorganizing the items on hangers, when there are no customers I amuse myself by watching, through the store window, seconds in the lives of people passing on the street. Inside, my gaze stops on each of the images that fill the shelves. The first photograph is a portrait, on foam board backing, of a couple in front of a horse. I imagine their real lives before and after the photograph. The man smiles with a triumphant air beside his girlfriend.

Their pastel-colored polo shirts are prominent in the scene. *She doesn't need money. She'll marry an important pharmaceutical executive, a friend of the family. Ten years later she has four children, she's gained weight and her husband is cheating on her with a younger woman. She decides to go back to school, etc.* The game requires avoiding clichés. Sometimes I'm better at it than other times. *The brown-haired guy with classical features is from a Belgian suburb, he was discovered by an agent at twenty-one, working behind the bar at a nightclub; now he earns much more than he'd ever dreamed of. Sometimes he is asked to escort ladies or gentlemen to parties. He'll be raped by a casting director. Eventually he'll be adopted by a businessman twenty years his senior, who unexpectedly makes him happy.*

I continue playing the game of reverse-characters, from photo to photo, until my gaze lands on the cotton Oxford shirts in shades of blue. The customers who buy them aren't like my father. My parents don't come into the store. I wouldn't either, I'd feel self-conscious. I started working for the company one year wrapping Christmas gifts in its discount store and a couple of months later I was transferred to the flagship store. The job offers more opportunity to let the mind wander than the restaurant business, where I had a boss who yelled at me when there were a lot of customers and I didn't run my tail off bringing out the dishes. To the left of the counter is the women's clothing, more colorful and varied in shape and texture. The more original pieces, the ones I would buy if I could afford them, rarely sell. Here people want to be cookie-cutter members of the happy club, filled with folks who go sailing or play golf; "If you want to be one of us, you must buy us," the polo players sewn onto the shirts whisper in chorus. The owner ignores my scant enthusiasm for sales because of my skill at dressing mannequins. After the four-hour morning shift and the four-hour afternoon shift, when I get home I will wait for everyone to have their dinner so I can use the kitchen table (the one in my room is too small, in the dining room the TV's always on). After wiping it down, I lay out my art-theory books. *Zeitgeist*, *Weltanschauung*, words with tiny footnotes. After a little while my eyelids grow heavy.

Opening up that first figurine by its narrow waist, the next one appears. Its features, ten years later, are now well-defined:

I am teaching behind glass walls. Through them influential parents, foreign teachers, and businessmen worried about the future of their family businesses, observe me, all of them paying close attention to the quality of service in a privileged, hothouse environment. This sort of atmosphere is prevalent uptown where, from kindergarten age, languages and future technologies are spoon-fed at breakfast. In this setting, egos – endowed with applause and medals for even the slightest achievement and from the earliest age – generally grow up with a very well developed sense of personal pride concerning themselves, even though not always toward others. *Because* – I thought – *if we changed the rules of this game and we all were dealt the same cards, or if at least there were rules that evened out the unequal distribution, if the playing field were neutral; if affection, the most highly valued asset in expensive schools (where all the rest is paid for with money) and all the other resources were available to everyone, perhaps then those who can't play now would play better* – she taught in various schools in less privileged areas, before finding a steady position at that school. She had seen a lot of talent wasted because it hadn't found the appropriate conditions, talent which that country seemed to only recognize early in the case of soccer players. Teaching according to new methods based on teamwork and projects, she saw how creative students were sometimes hampered by group negotiations monopolized by more dominant or extroverted students. *Teamwork is misunderstood* – I concluded after a time – *each student should be evaluated both for their ability to collaborate and for their individual contribution, which is made possible by the living dead who comprise the Canon; prior knowledge and the individual's contribution directed at the Contemporaries in a never-ending conversation: the reader collaborates; the group is made up of the reader, the author and author's influences that allowed him or her to create the work. What can emerge from that dialogue is also for others, perhaps not now, but maybe in the future it could take the shape of an artwork, or the ability to communicate in writing, or the development of a critical sensibility toward your surroundings, an ability that fuels the oft-trumpeted "innovation."*

I thought about all that, kept quiet and did my job the best I could in a competitive work environment because deep down, after some twisting to release it, figurine number three was still me:

Employee X who, as the business owner had accurately sensed, wouldn't make problems when she was let go. Because "you must have done something wrong if you're being punished," as Mother would say; and because "*you aren't a team player*," as Father would say in English. And being unemployed, was dating the third English teacher . . . *The Player, the Team*, and *the Punishment*, the rules of this pre-established game . . . The game in which the best card she had been dealt was one she herself had drawn and cut out. It would be best for her to focus on something she could put her faith in, even if that led her to an unknown place, while holding down a part-time job. She felt safer there than she had working for the editor, who expected her to go out to dinner with him after the commercial fairs, dinners that went on long and after which they had to head back to the hotel together. All that for eight hundred euros a month. So, she kept her job and, in her downtime, she poured a good deal of her energy into that place where Beauty, Truth, Play and Inventiveness should converge . . . Feeding this Project didn't help her pay the bills, which her family reproached her for, and later she would give in and start a full-time gig. While working full-time, the Project still called to her unceasingly; she would dedicate her nights, weekends, summers to it. Feeding it with the little time she had left meant renouncing other things in a feedback loop: in part she worked on the Project because she didn't have people to talk to, she didn't have them because she often shut herself in to work on the Project. It was the only complex way she had of expressing herself. She worked like a shipwreck on an iceberg island, without knowing where she was headed or how much longer she would be able to hold out. She had lost much of the determination needed to aspire to that uncomfortable word, somewhat ridiculous due to its extraordinarily wide range of meanings, from intellectual to starlet, meanings that often imply a life of partying and posturing, a life of improbable peaks and probable shipwrecks.

Shipwrecks where nobody, now that I'm an adult, is waiting to toss me a life vest.

The fourth figurine travels to the capital for her master's, falls in love with a charismatic professor and, thanks to the sophistry of the disenchanted Marxist who, feeding this all-too curious figurine's eagerness, manages to seduce her with the full consent of the adult she has now become, in a cyclical story like the Nietzschean eternal return that he himself teaches her. She falls deeply in love with the melancholic professor – or with his role, she'll never be entirely sure – as he teaches her first the theory and then the practice of the world; after some erectile problems, he abruptly says goodbye. He's suddenly forgotten the feminist rhetoric, and the eloquence and tact he employed to seduce her and others.

When you take hold of a drowning person's hand you run the risk of being pulled down beneath the waves; the survival instinct's movement is violent. Once under the water, with the cold, the electricity that lights up and connects the big, bright city that is the brain of a twenty-three-year-old begins to dim; the ideas that flowed, multiplying and interconnecting, freeze up. The refraction of that general blackout provokes a new opacity in the eyes, which had shone brightly up until then. Facial features grow heavy. Six times a day I repeat the same speech in front of different tourists. The same words, said over and over, lose their meaning. Reality dissolves. I can't explain what has happened. I have gaps in my memory. The water surrounding me slowly makes its way inside. I start to swell. Where did the darkness that drew me to him come from? Is it a familiar darkness? *I must have done something bad, otherwise this wouldn't be happening to me.*

The end of this sad, lonely period – the early twenties can be the loneliest time of your life – was when late-blooming acne and nearsightedness bad enough for glasses unscrewed to reveal a figurine marked by thicker outlines.

The fifth figurine believes that being invisible is the greatest power, not always getting what you want. Five extra kilos and short hair ward off complications; all that will save her problems during the four years she focuses on studying the art of telling lies in order to tell the truth. The poor girl whose story is always told by others, who liked to read Bolaño, Franzen and Zweig, who admired Duras, Némirovsky and Yourcenar, learns that an inexpressible story can kill the person who lived through it. Because those who cannot tell their own stories, or those who are silenced, are victims. This new voice will speak with authority, with full knowledge of what has attacked her on all sides. Because really she'd been stupid, it was stupid not to have taken advantage of what she had, for not realizing earlier that this world is brutal, that evil exists in people out of weakness and the thirst for power. Along with manipulation and gossip – the weapons of the weak – she could have used the few advantages of her gender, resources she had been taught to believe were shameful and superficial. She'd been raised by a strict mother as if evil could only emerge from within her. So she had painstakingly focused on the deep cleansing of her soul, she had worked hard to become as naïve and stupid as her brother, whom you could stop on the street and effortlessly relieve of the contents of his wallet; there's nothing like being dumb to allow you to observe others more clearly. That was how she tested out their principles, principles that are easy to forget when interacting with people like us, the simple, the wet behind the ears.

And then, in that calm period without any upsets, the once again narrow waist of the sixth figurine emerged:

A continuity assistant on a big-budget film. She carried a hidden camera. And the actors couldn't pose at their best angle, the one they offered up to the Director: that new panoramic shot revealed the lifts in the shoes of the short hero, the monster's zipper, and the gorgeous actress rewriting her script instead of being rescued. The only interest she might have had in filming that reverse angle wasn't about settling scores with anyone, nor fame – these days only money can save you and art offers little of that – but because she knew that the "off-camera" perspective fascinated many people, who feared the monster, admired the hero and waited for a rescue that never came. She thought that it was precisely when things get uncomfortable or can't be shown that something interesting comes to light. That is the point of no return, the point that must be reached, the point you reach after crossing the border of what has already been said, what has already been seen. It's cold out there.

Persevering and forging ahead to the blind spot completely surrounded by whiteness, the point from which you can see nothing and you don't know where to go, from that moment on, it is important to take measures, demarcate, and, even if just fumbling around in the dark, to correctly identify the origin and direction of the footprints.

It was by following that trail that I found, in the snow, much further on, the smallest figurine in the set, the one that isn't hollow but solid, the matrix whose expansion had generated the rest of the figurines and situations.

Research Notes I

PENGUINS

The penguins of the Antarctic were a new discovery for the explorers, who began filming them in the early twentieth century. Everyone was soon taken with the sweet creatures; people wanted to see images of the playful penguins. But if you've seen *Encounters at the End of the World*, by Werner Herzog, you'll know that sometimes a penguin will voluntarily separate from the group and head in the opposite direction, away from the sea, toward its death.

SOUTH POLE

There's a store downstairs on the street level that sells frozen foods. The cashier is tall, blond, stocky. He reminds me of Amundsen, the explorer.

PEAKS AND POLES

The Sherpas and the Inuit have similarities. The former reach the summit every day, the latter helped everyone discover the North Pole.

NEWS

The mountaineer Ferran Latorre gave up on his ascent of Everest in order to rescue a sick Sherpa.

THE WHITE RABBIT

When I was little, my mother worked in a small-town school. Its playground was the woods. Once I saw a bunny nestled among the roots of a tree. But it wasn't one of the typical rabbits that camouflage themselves amid the brown tones of the Mediterranean landscape; it was a white rabbit. When I got closer I saw that it was quite big; stock-still, it stared at me with its red eyes. It let me pick it up and I realized it was panting. I decided to take it to the vet, but on the way there, in the car, it died.

WHITE DEATH

Death by freezing is called sweet death, or white death. It is somehow linked to sleep, because of their apparent likeness, as opposed to the violence of a death by fire. Those who've seen it up close say that there's nothing sweet about an icy grave; freezing is as terrible a death as burning.

Yet ice retains the body's shape the way images do; it is like photographs. Photography is to its subject as ice is to the interred explorer: a thanatological process that presents us, abruptly, with a body from the past.

HONOR AND RECOGNITION

The white backdrop to polar explorations magnifies the already highly abstract nature of attempting to reach a geographic goal as intangible as a few coordinates on a map. What was it that led so many men to endeavor to conquer these vast white spaces devoid of any apparent commercial or strategic

Photograph of Robert Peary's arrival at the North Pole on April 21, 1909.

interest? What does such a conquest represent and how is it, in turn, represented?

While the historical research that makes up part of this investigation seemed to be a straight line leading to crystal-clear regions crowned with stories of scientific aplomb, it actually turned out to be meandering, and plagued by paradox and murkiness. The conquest of these last uncharted regions is so fascinating precisely because of its ambiguity, and because of its fertile hold on the popular imagination. One example: the conquest of the North Pole was attributed to Robert Edwin Peary in 1909. After twenty-three years of unsuccessful attempts, Peary pulled it off on his eighth try. Frederick Cook claimed he had reached the pole a year earlier. With no scientific means to prove who was the first to conquer the region, a dispute arose that captured the public interest. Popular opinion eventually shifted in Peary's favor, ruining Cook. When comparing the "conquest photographs" of each of the two explorers, there is no doubt as to who the winner would be. Peary's is shot from a low angle, and shows five men in front of a flag lodged in a carefully prepared mound of snow on the arctic plain. The staging, perfectly composed in the vast whiteness, excluded his most loyal companion, the African-American Matthew Henson. Cook's conquest was very different. With no one else to operate the camera, he photographed the pair of Inuits who traveled with him beside an igloo hoisting the inevitable flag over the arctic expanse. The resulting photograph is blurry.

Cook's photograph of his arrival at the North Pole, 1908.
Exact date unknown.

MAN IN ICE

My brother is a man trapped in ice. He looks at us through it; he is there and he is not there. Or more precisely, there is a fissure inside him that periodically freezes over. When he is present, his outline is more clearly defined; other times he's submerged for a while. His focus is at times ten thousand meters high (he likes to watch planes cross the sky) or, when the ice is thicker, ten thousand meters inward. In addition to planes, he's interested in trains, cars, dogs, cats, and birds. In his day-to-day life, the fissure within him leaves him stranded between one action and the next. But because his body is fully there, we have to make every decision for him. There is no outward indication of what's going on inside him. Disability is basically what hinders someone from being self-sufficient and having skills society is willing to pay for (if we take this less literally, it could include many of us); therefore, you could say that he is simply different, that he has other abilities: freelance air traffic controller, attentive observer of the local fauna, silent but present companion. The lack of external signs is somewhat disconcerting to strangers when they approach him and he responds in a stutter. Luckily he lives in a small city, he's known around the neighborhood and people generally take care of him if they come across him blocked, hesitating over crossing the street to drop the trash in the bin, one of his day's few moments, if not the only one, when he is by himself.

"How's it going?" I ask.

"Goodrealgood." It comes out all in a rush, his typical answer to that question.

M has a catalogue of responses that help him confront social situations. That is how he's learned to integrate into the world of others, a world where he has adapted over time, like a stranger in a distant land with an unfamiliar language. He knows that if everyone is laughing, he must laugh, and if everyone is serious he has to be serious. He only interrupts conversations in order to ask urgent and basic things, which he repeats in the same way each day at the same time:

"Should I go to the bathroom?" Right after meals.

"Should I drink water?" Once he's sat down at the table.

Having a son like this, let's be frank, is hard on my mother. I think sometimes she feels guilty, even though the origin of his problem is unclear. My mother and my brother, who is now grown-up and hairy (yet maintains a childlike innocence), have developed a certain interdependence. She hasn't had a serious relationship since splitting up with my father more than twenty years ago. So she is a polar conqueror and pulls my brother along on a toboggan.

As a boy it wasn't yet clear what was going on with him; at school he was just a bit behind in some aspects. Later the problem became more and more apparent. We don't know what caused it, whether it was due to a complication at birth – he was delivered via vacuum extraction, was it a question of not getting enough oxygen? – or if it's genetic, a thought that makes the idea of my having children fraught, even though there isn't another case in our family. Some research suggests that it has to do with the fertilizers that were used in the sixties and seventies, because there was an uptick in cases, but the increase could simply be due to the fact that they'd begun to diagnose it. The studies on autistic spectrum disorders don't clarify anything, and the doctors know very little. There are cases of genetically identical twins raised in the same home where one is autistic and the other isn't. The importance of the various environmental and genetic factors is still unknown, and there are no biological indicators that can detect the presence of autism after birth. That has weakened my trust in science: for years doctors have given my brother different names, depending on the pathological trend at the time: first he was borderline, from borderline he became Asperger, from Asperger to autistic, and now, since the classification encompasses so many different cases, it's called autism spectrum disorder (ASD). To me, this vague label seems like a path back toward uncertainty; the differences in behavior and appearance between the different cases are so vast that they often have very little in common.

When I came into the world, he was already there, and for many years his condition was an enigma, something unnamed. My older brother was diagnosed at the age of thirty. I was grateful to have a name for it, even one that isn't entirely apt. And I believe that I've been able to talk about it more since then. It is very important that things have a name, otherwise they don't exist.

The idea that the name often makes the thing is completely true.

COOK

Frederick Cook's polar obsession started when his first wife and their baby son died during the birth. It was as a surgeon on one of Robert Peary's expeditions that the doctor began his explorations. The so-called "polar controversy" took place when, years later and on different expeditions, in 1909 Peary

"The Conquest of Mount McKinley" by Frederick Cook is the most controversial photograph in the history of polar exploration.

and Cook returned at the same time from the Arctic claiming to have been the first to reach the North Pole. One of the documents that Cook brought back from the expedition was the photograph of his companion reaching the summit of Mount McKinley, the highest peak in Alaska, which is actually still quite far from the North Pole. Peary was convinced that the photograph had been retouched, and thus began the first argument questioning his adversary's honesty, as a means to call into question his having made it to the North Pole. In the photograph the shape of the peak had been modified by cropping both sides of the mountain to accentuate the steepness of the slope. Even though several expeditions of the period sought to confirm its veracity, the weather conditions made it impossible to recreate a photograph from the same angle to determine the facts.

RECROPPING HISTORY Scholars now believe that a picture of Dr. Frederick Cook that appeared in "To the Top of the Continent" in 1908 purporting to show him atop Mount McKinley was actually taken 19 miles away atop Fake Peak. The image was cropped to eliminate evidence of the location.

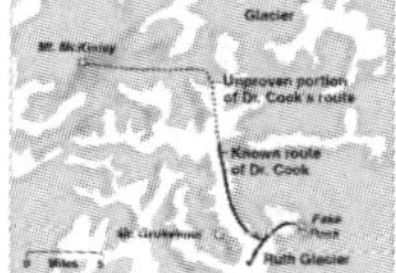

Later, Cook gave conferences depicting himself as a misunderstood man who had been robbed of his glory by Peary's influential circle of friends. He even went so far as to make a film, *The Truth About the Pole* (1912), that shows, above all, the scant means needed to represent life at the poles: a wood cabin on a white background tells his version of the events. The dispute continued until the United States entered World War I and public curiosity in the polar question waned and Cook turned his eye to oil speculation, for which he was accused of fraud and ended up in prison. After his release in 1930, he tried to again stake his claim as the first conqueror of the pole, but the scientific committees no longer took him seriously.

BELOW

Every month all the things we couldn't buy, and we won't buy in the months to come, end up somewhere, out, under the ice. The platonic loves form into crystals and also get stuck beneath the snow. Unfulfilled desires, when they accumulate, cause cracks that appear on the forehead. Sometimes we slip on the ice and fall into deeper crevasses. After a long time there can be a thaw and everything below emerges like the mammoths on the Siberian plains in summer. The remains are damp and smelly. Then we no longer want them. We think they're not worth it. Money wasted or love squandered on the undeserving.

The desires frozen for lack of money or unrequited love are different from the ones we freeze because we've given up on them. The latter have the gleam of stoic heroism. Even though we might be renouncing our desires out of fear, and we'll spend our lives blind, without feeling or seeing anything . . . On the other hand, if we obey our desires we could end up lost. What makes Odysseus a hero is that he renounces and does not renounce. When he allows himself to listen to the sirens' song, he remains careful but allows himself his desire.

Captain Shackleton and his entire crew suffered a shipwreck while trying to cross the Antarctic. They were adrift for months, hearing the song of the orcas; his feat, like Odysseus's, was returning home. But there on solid ground something sank inside the captain – the domestic realm can be the most difficult territory to settle – and in 1920, just three years after having miraculously escaped death several times, Shackleton abruptly announced that he needed to return to one of the polar regions. He didn't care whether it was the North Pole or the South.

COOK, PEARY, AND THE TRUTH

I imagine the moment in the early twentieth century when an explorer puts down his compass – which spins, lost, at the poles – and makes observations on his position, then decides to plant a flag in the middle of a field of white.

> The Pole at last!!! The prize of three centuries, my dream and ambition for twenty-three years. *Mine at last . . .*
>
> ROBERT PEARY

According to many documents that can be found on the internet, Peary was the first to reach the North Pole. Frederick Cook is depicted as the imposter who used fake evidence to claim he had got there a year earlier. Currently most studies conclude that neither of them ever really reached the Pole. Peary's assertions have been challenged for the following reasons: a) in the small group that traveled with Peary, there was no one with sufficient navigational knowledge to independently confirm their position; b) the speeds that Peary claimed to have hit on his return were three times faster than on his way there; c) his account of a straight route to the Pole and back – the only way he could have done it – is contradicted by Matthew Henson's description of a tortuous detour. In 1996 a analysis of some Peary's records was carried out, using new scientific knowledge. It indicated that Peary was almost 37 kilometers from the Pole.

Laurell Hamilton described Cook's situation in these words: "If people will not believe the truth, and you don't want to lie, then you're out of options."

The Truth About The Pole (1912). Still from the film by Frederick Cook.

In the United States there are still those who defend Cook as the true discoverer of the North Pole (Frederick A. Cook Society http://www.cookpolar.org).

S.O.S. EISBERG

Once I was into a guy who wasn't into me. That made me like him even more. After a while, his absolutely indifferent attitude toward me made my attraction shift into fascination; an image I could moon over, fully aware I was being masochistic.

Sometimes I imagined that he knew, and that his behavior was caused by something keeping him from getting closer to me, perhaps some obligation I was oblivious to, some mission he had to accomplish before he could return. Like an explorer's wife, I waited for him. I dubbed him Iceberg, believing I could only see one ninth of him. Icebergs have a sublime, dangerous beauty; they can sink a ship. There are also moments in which my fantasizing stopped and I simply felt disgust at my attraction to that being who was so icy and insensitive, at least toward me.

Some time later I experienced one of those loves that make you understand the meaning of the word home. I stopped thinking about him, but sometimes I still dreamed about him. In the dreams he was distant too. The Arctic is etymologically the land of the bear. It is there where I situated Iceberg's geography. He was, in fact, a tall, solitary, and phlegmatic man.

S.O.S. Eisberg. Arnold Fanck (1933), with Leni Riefenstahl.

THE FROZEN EXPLORERS

On January 17, 1912, Scott reached the South Pole. The photograph he took there documents his failure – arriving in second place – after Amundsen got there on December 15, 1911. It is a full shot of a group of men, isolated on the Antarctic plain, in profile before a tent that flies a Norwegian flag. The photograph of Scott, who arrived a month too late and found proof of his defeat, documents his own bleak state. The comparison between the photographs is terrible: the victory is cold and the defeat is epic.

The race between Roald Amundsen and Robert Falcon Scott to conquer the South Pole ended in tragedy. Scott and his expedition companions died of cold and hunger on their way back to the base.

According to Amundsen's diary, on December 14, 1911 they reached the spot where his previous calculations had indicated the South Pole was located. They took precise solar measurements to be certain of their position. Meanwhile they decided to travel a certain extra distance in the three remaining directions from that camp, omitting only the direction they'd come from. A different direction was assigned to each member of the team and they headed out without resting for twenty more kilometers. They were risking their lives in this operation; without navigational instruments, a storm could easily have led them astray and they would have been lost forever. The next day they returned almost simultaneously after covering those forty kilometers. While they were gone, Amundsen and Hanssen had been able to make more accurate measurements, which confirmed that they were still a few kilometers from the Pole. With this information, they estimated the correct direction and covered the remaining distance in one day. They camped at the location that, according to their instruments, could be considered the South Pole. Then on December 17, Hanssen and Bjaaland again covered seven kilometers in another direction to ensure that they had reached the South Pole.[1]

According to various polar historians, Amundsen's success lies in his use of skis and above all to his embracing of Inuit expertise. Amundsen was pragmatic, even eating his dogs when necessary. Scott's aversion to sacrificing dogs led him to instead bring ponies, although he refused to kill them as well, even when his companions were starving to death. So Scott's story reveals the contradictions of a character who, while on the one hand seeming to be a model of ambition and perseverance, on the other, some say, represents the height of incompetence. The especially low temperatures in the region when they set off on their return trip were another hurdle.

1 Amundsen's conquest seems so formal and unheroic, with its constant measuring and corrections, like the process of writing and editing a text . . .

When he realized on the way back that he would soon starve, Scott wrote to his wife: "I had to force myself into being strenuous, as you know – had always an inclination to be idle." Close to death he seems satisfied: "What lots and lots I could tell you of this journey. How much better it has been than lounging about in too great comfort at home."

The corpses of Scott and his four companions were found some months later, in November of 1912, with the expedition diaries intact: "These rough notes and our dead bodies must tell the tale."

The inscription on the cross marking the spot where Captain Scott and his companions died is a quote from the poem "Ulysses" by Tennyson: "To strive, to seek, to find, and not to yield." This heroic epitaph is much more sympathetic to the heroes when we look at it in more context:

> It may be that the gulfs will wash us down:
> It may be we shall touch the Happy Isles,
> And see the great Achilles, whom we knew.
> Tho' much is taken, much abides; and tho'
> We are not now that strength which in old days
> Moved earth and heaven, that which we are, we are;
> One equal temper of heroic hearts,
> Made weak by time and fate, but strong in will
> To strive, to seek, to find, and not to yield.

Amundsen's victory. December 14, 1911. Photograph by Olav Bjaaland.

Scott's defeat, January 17, 1912.

Research Notes II

EPIC I

Is it possible for an epic to not be imperialist, athletic, or totalitarian?

EPIC II

Isn't there a territorial struggle in every family story? Domestic and emotional spaces as territories to be conquered.

AHAB

Sometimes I feel like Captain Ahab, pursuing my white whale. With me is E, who, like Ishmael, is spectator to an obsession he does not always understand.

ZEPPELIN

As for Peary, some historians believe that he truly thought he had reached the Pole. Others have suggested that he purposely exaggerated his feat. There are those who say that any and all indications that Peary didn't reach the North Pole are the discrediting work of conspirators in favor of Cook.

Each of the men mounted a publicity campaign, resulting in a very public face-off. They were both convinced of their version of the facts, but in an age without the technical means to verify them.

In 1926, the members of Amundsen's expedition by dirigible were the first to unquestionably see the North Pole as they flew over it. On the other hand, the first to set foot there with any proof were the twenty-four scientists under Aleksandr Kuznetsov's command who reached the Pole by plane in 1948 under Stalin's orders. And it wasn't until 1969, the same year as the moon landing, when an expedition headed by Wally Herbert got there without mechanical means, by sled.

Conquering the North Pole had been a dream for centuries, but as the Arctic historian Christopher Pala said, those who achieved it weren't those who had been dreaming of it.

Norge airship.
Amundsen-Ellsworth-Nobile Expedition, 1926.

Research Notes III

THURSDAY, AUGUST 16, 2012

I've found the southernmost Spanish scientist. During the winter months in the Antarctic he and a few colleagues will be alone there maintaining the Amundsen-Scott South Pole Station.

Reading his blog, I find this:

> Today, to welcome in the civil twilight and bid farewell to the nautical twilight, I went for a walk. In each of the four directions (N, S, E, W), there are a series of panels that serve to check visibility in the summer for arriving flights. To the east, the first one is half a mile away. From there you can see the next one, a mile away from the base. When you get there you can see the next one, a mile and a half out. My heart started to beat faster because the base already seemed distant. I was tempted to go on. When I got to the third one, I could see the fourth and last one another half-mile ahead, so I continued. It was spectacular, and a bit unsettling, when I turned around and could no longer see the base, which was two miles away. There was no sign of any geographical feature or texture; it was all uniform, white.

Beautiful. Soon, since I knew where to look, I figured out more or less where I was. In any case, I could follow my footprints back. Out there I couldn't hear a thing, except for the whistling in my ears. There was barely any wind. Total solitude.[2]

[2] Carlos Pobes. Facebook status update from September 6, 2012. The author's website: http://www.eldiamaslargodemivida.com/es.

ATLAS CRYSTAL WORKS

The snow globe had been left at the back of a drawer in an old dresser in the rented apartment. I put it on my desk on a pile of papers – research documents of my white obsessions – as a paperweight. Inside there are two innocently imprisoned angels, who pray half-naked as if the water and floating snow had nothing to do with them. The glass sphere rests on a plastic book, a miniature Bible. I wish the globe was empty; I express that desire to the internet. I find some factories in the United States that make them to order, you can even put a photo inside. According to the website, there is little written on the history of snow globes but it seems the first ones were made in France in the nineteenth century. This object could have been conceived as a successor to the glass paperweight – another fascinating object – that was popular in previous eras.

Snow globes arrived en masse during the 1878 World Fair in Paris. They became the souvenir of choice of those attending. At that time, at least five American companies were producing snow globes and selling them to Europe. A snow globe containing a model of the newly built Eiffel

Tower was made for the 1889 Fair, in commemoration of one hundred years since the French Revolution. The image of a snow globe with a tiny guillotine inside runs fleetingly through my mind.

Snow globes became popular in England during the Victorian era. In the early twenties they gained traction in the United States among collectors. Many of them were made by the Atlas Crystal Works. In the United States, during the forties, snow globes were often used as an advertising tool. In Europe, during the forties and fifties, globes with religious scenes became a common gift for Catholic children. Snow globes have made appearances in many films and were a key visual motif in *Citizen Kane* (1941). After saying "Rosebud," Kane drops the snow globe and dies. It had been a gift from his former lover Susan and held a humble log cabin, his childhood home.

When snow globes contain human figures instead of buildings or objects, they give the sinister, damp sensation of containing people imprisoned and tossed out to sea.

I search for the Atlas Crystal Works factory online. I find an address:

425 E Pleasant Ave., Covington, TN 38019 (901) 476-9797
Covington, Tennessee, USA

The famous factory that produced so many snow globes, right around the time that *Citizen Kane* was filmed, is in Tennessee, in the American South. Google Street View shows a small white industrial unit on a street of low houses with porches.

The kind of house in the deep South where little Mick lived, the girl from *The Heart is a Lonely Hunter* by Carson McCullers, a novel published during the height of snow globes' popularity. McCullers's debut is usually described as fiction that deals with the spiritual isolation of misfits and the marginalized in the American South during the thirties. The gallery of opaque lives that fills the novel includes the deaf-mute Singer; Copeland, the doctor who fruitlessly tries to free his fellow negroes from slavery through education; and Mick, a girl who likes jazz, smokes in secret, and dropped out of school to work:

> Sometimes it was like she was out in Switzerland and all the mountains were covered with snow and she was skating on cold, greenish-colored ice. Mister Singer would be skating with her. And maybe Carole Lombard or Arturo Toscanini who played on the radio. They would be skating together and then Mister Singer would fall through the ice and she would dive in without regard for peril and swim under the ice and save his life. That was one of the plans always going on in her mind.

McCullers presents us with her characters' mute struggle to emerge on the surface and breathe. I look for snow globes from the forties, when the novel was just published. I find a few, made at the Atlas Crystal Works factory, on a website devoted to second-hand sales. I notice that in most of the old snow globes the water level has decreased. There is one that holds a figure of a black servant woman. The inscription on the base reads "Just a Little Mammy Down in Dixie."[3] The seller of this antique informs potential buyers that the water might be a bit murky because of dissolved "snow," which was made from sawdust or bone shavings before they started making it from plastic. Inside the snow globe the level of the liquid is now at the figure's shoulders, so her head emerges.

I wonder at what point in history this woman began to "breathe."

[3] http://www.atomicmall.com/view.php?id=Mammy-Snow-Globe-Atlas-Crystal-Works_884055.

SHACKLETON

After the conquest of the North Pole by Peary and the South Pole by Amundsen, there were no conquests left for the British nation. Ernest Shackleton, who had traveled with Captain Scott during the *Discovery* expedition (1900–1904) to the North Pole, thought up a new challenge for the heroic age of discovery:

> From the sentimental point of view, it is the last great Polar journey that can be made. It will be a greater journey than the journey to the Pole and back, and I feel it is up to the British nation to accomplish this, for we have been beaten at the conquest of the North Pole and beaten at the conquest of the South Pole. There now remains the largest and most striking of all journeys – the crossing of the Continent.

Captain Shackleton's expedition (1914–1917) named his ship *Endurance*, in reference to his family motto "Fortitudine Vincimus," which means: "Through Endurance, We Conquer." Beyond the conquest of new lands and the encounters with dangerous enemies, this was a journey into extreme weather conditions. As the ship's name indicates, this was a feat that would put the crew's physical and psychological endurance to the test.

Before setting off on their adventure, the personal diaries and images of the crew members had already been sold; Shackleton encouraged the twenty-seven crewmen to keep a journal on the ship. The expedition would be documented by Australian photographer Frank Hurley.

The ship captained by Shackleton set off toward Antarctica in August 1914. After more than eight months of sailing, they reached the cold southernmost seas; the deeper they got into the Weddell Sea, the slower they moved: immense masses of ice weighing thousands of tons blocked their way.

> At seven in the evening, Greenstreet steered the *Endurance* between two large icebergs toward a stretch of open water. Halfway there, the ship hit one of the bergs and the other closed it in from behind. [. . .] Six cold, cloudy days passed before the sky cleared on January 24. By that point, the *Endurance* was already surrounded by ice on all sides.[4]

They were trapped for some eight months. Finally, on October 27, 1915, the wooden hull of the *Endurance* began to crack, making a sound similar to cannon balls crashing into the ship. A dejected Shackleton ordered his men to abandon ship. From that moment on the crew was adrift in lifeboats or on ice floes, until they reached Elephant Island on August 30, 1916.

[4] Caroline Alexander, *The Endurance: Shackleton's Legendary Antarctic Expedition.*

After losing hope of rescue from Elephant Island, Shackleton set sail with five men in a small boat, seven meters long, the *James Caird*, to search for help on South Georgia Island, located 1,300 kilometers away. Sailing through twelve-meter-high waves for fourteen days, they finally managed to reach terra firma. When they got to South Georgia, they realized they were at the island's south coast, which was uninhabited. The two extremes of the island are separated by a mountain chain with peaks higher than 3,000 meters, which at that point were yet to be explored. Three of the five men undertook this second journey, without any equipment. They added a few nails from the ship to the soles of their shoes and headed off through the mountains and glaciers without even stopping to sleep. The journey took thirty-six hours and Shackleton, who did not consider himself a believer, declared that he felt they were accompanied by a fourth traveler. After a difficult descent that included climbing down a frozen waterfall, they could make out the whaling port of Husvik. Once there, they were able to ask for help, though the challenging weather meant the first three rescue attempts, with three different vessels, failed. The British Government was busy with World War I and did not send aid. Finally they made it on the fourth try, with a ship they'd rented at Punta Arenas, Chile, rescuing the remaining twenty-two crew members, all still alive. By that time, those on the expedition had spent nine months surrounded by ice in the most adverse of conditions. In a letter to his wife, Shackleton wrote: "Damn the Admiralty. I wonder who is responsible for their attitude to me. Not a life lost and we have been through Hell."

ARTIFICIAL SNOW

The young nuclear physicist Ukichiro Nakaya arrived at the University of Hokkaido in 1932. Hokkaido is the northernmost island of Japan, and as such the closest to the Okhotsk Sea. The Physics Department had meager research funds and equally scant facilities. The only thing they seemed to have in abundance on Hokkaido was ice. In fact today it is known as a skiing destination. Taking advantage of what was on hand, Nakaya began to research ice crystals. Snow forms in nature when a drop of water or steam freezes inside a cloud around a suspended particle (such as a bit of dust or pollen). When frozen, the drop of water becomes a crystal in the shape of a hexagonal prism. This transition process is called "reverse sublimation" and describes the direct conversion from the gaseous state of the steam to the solid state of the snow crystals. Snow can form in the atmosphere at or below 0°C when there is a minimum of humidity. It is never too cold for snow; it forms at extremely low temperatures. The six arms of a snow crystal reflect the internal order of water molecules. Which is why the six points of the hexagon appear in the process of crystallization. The way these branches grow depends on the atmospheric conditions (temperature, pressure, amount of water . . .), and that variation leads the flakes to take on semi-random shapes that are always different; there are no two identical snowflakes. They typically measure about a centimeter and a half, even though there are recorded cases of snowflakes as big as five centimeters in diameter. The first person who photographed these crystals was Wilson Bentley, a farmer in Vermont, in 1885. After many unsuccessful attempts, Bentley managed to attach a microscope to a camera in order to capture the phenomenon. He amassed a collection of 5,000 images, and is the father of photomicrography, the photography of objects invisible to the naked eye.

Ukichiro Nakaya in his laboratory, 1938.

Nakaya took three thousand photomicrographs of snow crystals, allowing him to establish a general classification of the shapes, which he subdivided into forty-one types.

One day in his lab, Ukichiro Nakaya found a snowflake on the tip of a rabbit hair on his jacket. As if in a strange variation on Alice's search, it was a rabbit – albeit a dead one sewn onto a coat – that pointed the way toward the creation of artificial snow. Following its trail, the young scientist copied the temperature and humidity conditions in his laboratory at the moment the snowflake formed. On March 12, 1936, Nakaya created the first artificial snowflake, again on a rabbit hair. Up until that point, there had been numerous famous scientists and philosophers who had taken an interest in the phenomenon of snow crystals. The first ones were described by the Chinese in the second century BC. Subsequent attempts to address this problem in a more systematic way were carried out by the scientific philosophers of the seventeenth century in the West. Johannes Kepler began in 1611 with his treatise "On the Six-Cornered Snowflake," followed by Descartes, and then Robert Hooke, who enjoyed the advantages of the latest technological advance – the microscope – and to whom we owe the first detailed drawings.

In *The Spiritual History of Ice: Romanticism, Science, and the Imagination* – whose title sums up my fascinations of the last two years – Eric G. Wilson speaks about the strange obsession of some thinkers with snowflakes: Emanuel Swedenborg, a hero of the Romantics who spoke with angels, began his career as a crystallographer. He had the theory that ice crystals reveal the inner laws of the universe. In 1721, before his attentions became captivated by heavens and hells, Swedenborg wrote *The Principles of Chemistry*. In this work he put forth a theory that was taken up by eighteenth- and early-nineteenth-century scientists: the tiny geometries of snowflakes are portals to the essence of the cosmos. Thoreau concluded that the crystals, despite their cold geometry, are emanations of a vital principle, thus he perceived a comfortable regularity in the crystals' delicate structure; the world as a geometric organ.

Nakaya described his first experiments with snow in this way:

> I recall that, in our artificial snow experiments, there were some failures. We were therefore delighted to find similar mishaps in natural snow. In preparing papers for presentation we select only the photographs of well-formed crystals we have made, but in fact there were, and still are, a considerable number of failures. There are times when a crystal that starts on the right track will suddenly make an unexpected turn and assume a shape that defies any attempt at categorization. Such oddities that cannot be identified as crystals are considered failures, and we must start all over again.
>
> However, if you look at natural snow with that perspective, you can find similar weird forms. After you discover one irregularity you notice others, one after another, at various stages of development, showing that natural snow is also capable of failure – to our great relief.
>
> Once I came upon a most marvelous example of failed development in natural snow and cried out, "Come look,

another mistake!" My assistant Mr. H. peered into the microscope and his face lit up with a blissful smile.[5]

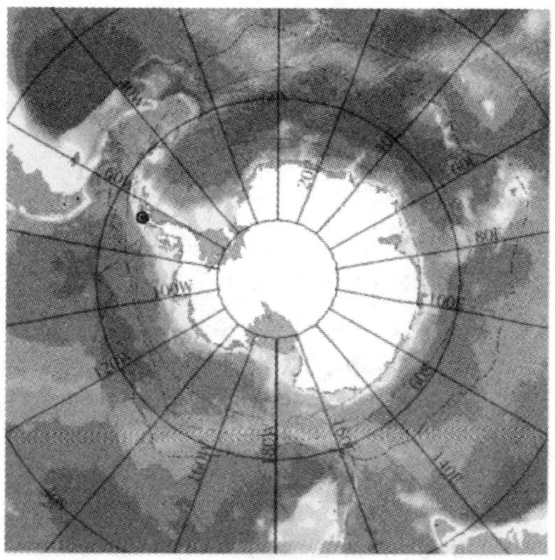

The islands of Antarctica named after Nakaya.

Ukichiro Nakaya had three daughters: Fujiko, Sakiko, and Miyoko. Fujiko Nakaya, born in Sapporo, Hokkaido, in 1933, is an artist known for her sculptural fog installations, or environments, that she began making in the seventies. Going against her father's geometric order, Fujiko enlisted the same medium, water vapor, to create spaces where geometry is erased and shapes lose their name.

[5] Ukichiro Nakaya, an excerpt from *Snow Postscripts*. Translation by Keiko Murata.

MAN IN ICE II

Unlike the clichés about autism, my brother doesn't hit his head against walls or avoid physical contact. He's simply passive; when he's hungry he doesn't go to the fridge, and when he's tired he doesn't go to bed. If we didn't tell him what to do, he would remain blocked indefinitely. So, from when he gets up until when he goes to sleep, he has to be told to do every action, or it has to be done for him. We don't know what is going on inside of him. It seems to me that in his brain the fissure is an obstacle between the I and the you, between one action and the next. Like a video streaming online, when the internet connection isn't fast enough, sometimes his actions freeze up. The doctor told us about a problem with neurotransmitters that makes him unable to hug us or ask how we are. It means it takes him at least half an hour to tie his shoes. It means that he might stop in the middle of closing a door. M stutters, as if there were also snow between one syllable and another.

"Mo-mo-mo-mo-mom, should I go to the bathroom?"

He stutters, on average, about four times before saying the whole word. When he eats a salad, he leaves the olive pits lined up, one by one, on the side of the plate. At the end of the meal we have: his plate and cup lined up, his silverware parallel at the same distance, olive pits in a line perpendicular to the silverware and at the height of the cup forming a horizontal line. Pure constructivism.

THE HEROIC AGE

The so-called heroic age of polar expedition – taken as stretching from the last decade of the nineteenth century to Captain Shackleton's death in 1922 – coincided with the development of photographic cameras and the invention of cinema, so it's not surprising that many polar explorers saw the potential of this new medium as a research tool. There are a series of films from this period, though they've received little attention from historians of documentary film. Unlike other, more recent conquests – like the conquest of space – the polar explorers left behind a large quantity of documents of unquestionable scientific value, which often are testament to the literary talents of their authors. One of the survivors of the *Terra Nova* expedition to Antarctica (1911–1912), Apsley Cherry-Garrard said: "Exploration is the physical expression of the Intellectual Passion."

This age of polar exploration basically began in order to showcase nations' achievements. The conquest of a moving point became a race, sometimes with rather dubious scientific aims. The representation of man in a hostile environment was depicted romantically; the sublime landscapes were the backdrop to a masculine epic journey whose only enemy was the harsh weather.

Both the Inuit guides, who led so many men to the North Pole, and the women, who waited, accompanied or spurred on the expeditions, got left somewhere beneath the snow.

Research Notes IV

AUGUST 26, 2012

Neil Armstrong, the first man to set foot on the Moon, has died. His obituary says that it is our mission to conquer Mars for the coming generations.

AUGUST 27, 2012

It's hot but I'm talking about snow.

AUGUST 30, 2012

News item:

Today Scott's ship, the *Terra Nova*, was found in Greenland. Some scientists who were carrying out underwater tests with sonar detected an object fifty-seven meters long. One of them, a fan of the history of that expedition, suspected that it could be the famed boat that left England to conquer the South Pole. The article has an embedded video. In it, you can blurrily watch a probe exploring a very dark marine floor. At first all you see are well-lit plankton particles, eventually very decomposed pieces of wood appear.

Disturbing the *Terra Nova* in its white tomb seems like sacrilege to me.

SEPTEMBER 15, 2012

Lately something unprecedented has been happening: my brother, who is generally passive and calm, gets enraged when he can't unbutton his pants, or shave himself. Then he picks up whatever's nearby, throws it, and cries. Only my mother has seen it happen; she told me about it recently, with concern.

My brother will outlive my parents, who fear for his future. Making sense of all this, when you don't believe in God, is difficult. I imagine my brother in other time periods, in other families. Would the Inuit have abandoned him on the ice? Would he have lived to middle age? Would he have been put in an institution, fifty years ago? What responsibility do I have in all this?

NOVEMBER 12, 2012

News item:

Two people die, an eighty-two-year-old mother and her forty-year-old daughter. The mother's death from natural causes is followed by her disabled daughter's death: of starvation. Did they live alone, isolated, at the North Pole? No, they lived in my country.

MISS BOYD LAND

In 1955 Louise Boyd became the first woman to fly over the Earth's rotational axis. At sixty-eight years old, she hired a private plane with expert pilots and headed for the North Pole. This wasn't the whim of a rich old lady; since 1926, she had led seven polar expeditions of great geographic, scientific and strategic value. Boyd, whose last name is reminiscent of "void," explored still-unknown corners of the Arctic map. She specialized in the northeastern region and in the sea floor of Greenland, which she measured and photographed with the era's most modern technology. To show their appreciation, the Danish government named a region of the Arctic that she discovered Louise Boyd Land. Her publications, photographs and films are still used today to evaluate the effects of climate change on the Arctic.

Born in San Rafael, California, the daughter of gold-mine owners, Louise grew up in Marin County, north of San Francisco, with her two brothers, Seth and John. When she was a teenager, both her brothers died of heart disease in a short span of time. Her parents were devastated and invested all their hopes in their daughter.

At twenty-two she was already heading up the family investment company. At thirty, in 1919, Louise bought a car and crossed the entire United States in an era when there were no highways and many roads were still unpaved. Her parents both died soon after, before 1920 was out. Rich and orphaned, she threw herself into the social scene. But she soon grew bored with that, and the dream that she'd had since childhood of seeing the North kept coming back. In 1924, she set out on a series of trips to the Arctic, starting in Norway, where for the first time she saw the fjords touching the polar cap. In that journey to the coasts of Spitsbergen, when she glimpsed the masses of ice in the distance, she said: "I want to be there, looking out, instead of out here looking in." Am I looking out or am I looking in? I wonder, as I see myself reflected in those words. Are we reading ourselves, when we read others? Are we looking in or out when we write?

I go back to the facts and the documents: one of her photographs on the internet shows a glacier flanked by two mountains. The white tongue that slides between them transcends the coldness of the frozen matter; its sinuous form – semi-liquid, semi-solid – slithers along, like a silent, sexual licking of the known world by the uncharted.

Boyd was drawn to the conquest of the void. In this photograph the victor is the unknown, indeed the immeasurable, which invades the solidity of the landscape.

This epic voyage to delimit the abyss by someone who had lost all points of reference highlights the foundational nature of house and family, as a centripetal or centrifugal force. Like a home, like a refuge, like a battlefield, or like a haunted house.

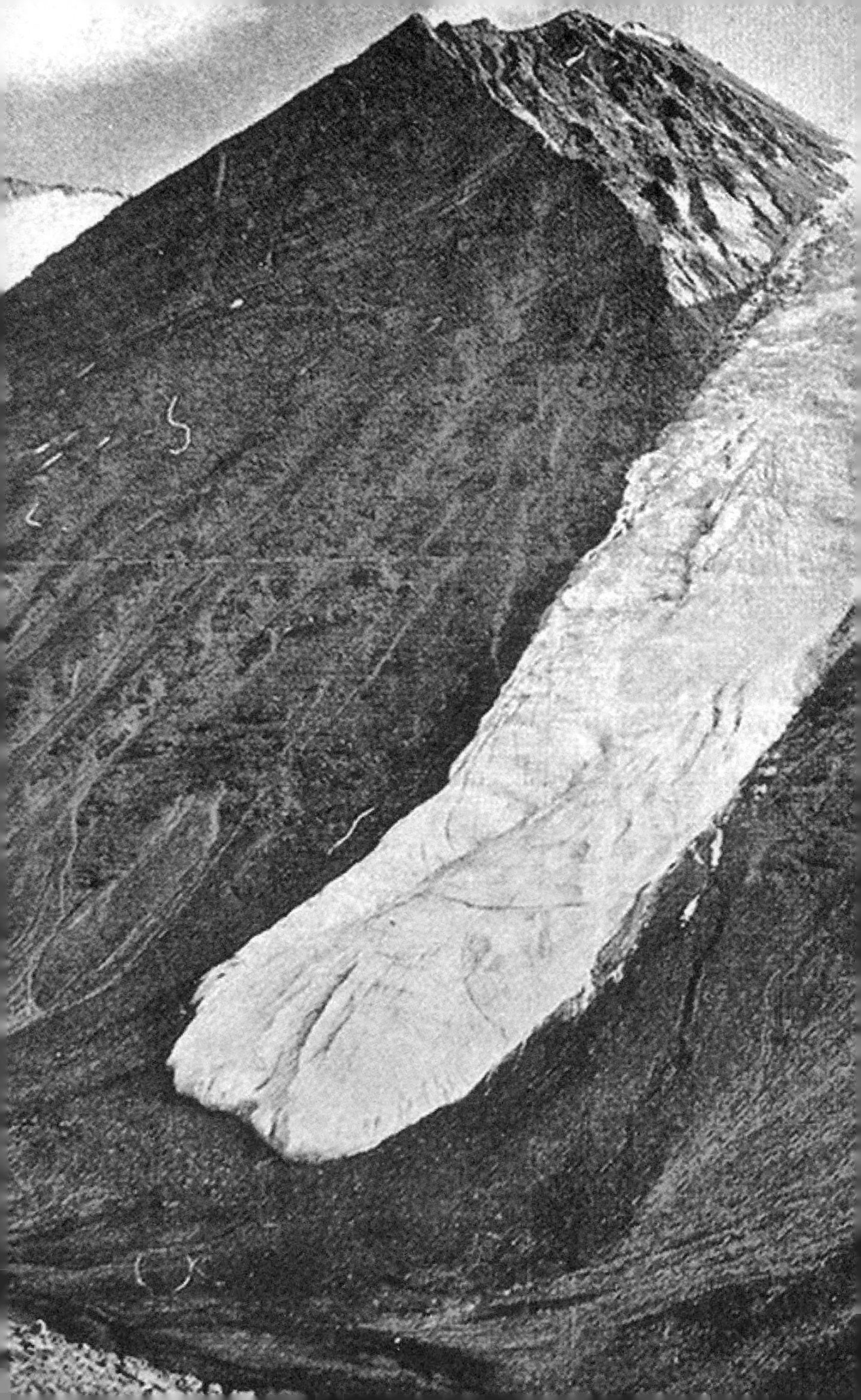

PHOTOGRAPH BY LOUISE BOYD

THE CONTINUITY OF POOLS

Secretly I've always thought that all the swimming pools in the world are interconnected. Depending on the hemisphere where they're located, their waters filter through underground veins toward the Arctic continent or Antarctica. The melting of the floes brings them back together and sends them into the sea, where they gather in desalination plants before finally returning to ponds, reservoirs, and municipal pools. That same water is filtered through us daily, making up seventy percent of our bodies. Imbibed and instinctively expelled to the tune of two liters a day, it leaves us through our urine, tears, excrement, saliva, sweat, and the steam we exhale through our mouths and skin. Each of our eighty-six billion brain cells is made up primarily of liquid, without which we would progressively lose consciousness. So we could say that our consciousness is comprised of seventy percent water; oceans, lakes, rivers, pools continue through us and filter into the depths of our thought. The other thirty percent – permanent dry residue – is completely renewed every seven years. Hardly anything remains of you besides the continuity of your history, that which you manage to retain despite the constant pillaging of your physical body, an extremely fragile, permeable barrier that is traversed each and every day by rivers, waterfalls, continents, multitudes.

THE ICEBREAKER

I often find myself getting stuck in this project. I see nothing before me, just white. Yet beneath it there are many things. The shrieking of seals. Was it the poles I wanted to talk about? Or is it just the image of the snow that fascinates me? Instability, confusion, cold (it's hot), determination. Sensations that were the constant companions of the polar explorers, as well as those of us who work with the blank white page. Because I'm not interested in the polar explorers in and of themselves, but rather in the idea of investigation, of seeking out something in an unstable space. I'd like to talk about all that as a metaphor, because what interests me is the possibility of an epic, a new epic, without foes or enemies; an epic involving oneself and an idea. Like the epic that artists and writers undertake.

Some mountaineers have reached their highest peaks after a severe personal crisis, when they found themselves stuck at a dead end. That reminds me of the epic of remaining in the place where we are and enduring what life has dealt us. Yes, that is also epic: not fleeing but staying put – I think of my mother, of so many who take care of dependent parents and children – and of anyone who resists in an intractable situation, like an illness. And that is epic, it is a battle. But there aren't yet good images or good metaphors for all that.

I am searching for them.

Research Notes V

HEROES

The question in *Fitzcarraldo*, Herzog's film in which the protagonist ascends a mountain in a steamship to descend on the other side, is whether we are dealing with a hero or an antihero. This question runs through most of my readings on conquests and explorations, when looking at the personal biographies of Amundsen, Boyd, Cook, Peary, Shackleton, Scott.

IN CLASS

Today in class, with my students, we were writing a story about a man in love with a hippopotamus. One of them declared: "It should be a walrus, they're harder to kiss."

CONQUERORS

At my high school there was a sign that said: "The world belongs to those who read."

That's a lie, I think, a big fat lie.

I seek. I don't know when I will return. I'll bring back the goods, but I don't know when.[6]

[6] "Hunter" by Björk plays in the background.

THE METHOD

My brother has taught me many things, starting when I was very small. When we had coloring books, I'd fill them quickly with a scribble on each page, while he patiently and systematically colored over my scribble, as if my mark weren't even there. That enraged me and at the same time amazed me. Similarly, he always finished the sticker albums I left half-done. I've always been irritated by systematization, because it goes against my nature, but later, seeing the results it brings, I've attempted it. In the end I've become someone who scribbles, systematically.

II

LIBRARY ATOP AN ICEBERG

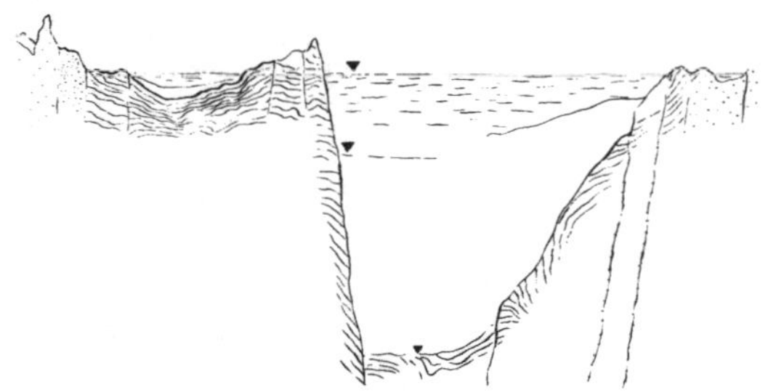

THE FAULT

I'm eight years old. One day when I come home from school, I find my parents waiting for me in the dining room. I sit on my father's lap. I don't really understand what they are saying. They explain that I'll have two homes, that my dad's going to buy us a VCR. Even though they try to put an optimistic spin on the situation, they don't seem happy. My brother accepts it calmly, I cry.

The first Christmas I find green pills in the kitchen, at the bottom of drawers, and in my mother's purse.

My father starts to wear jeans and cowboy boots. He asks the clerks in a record store what music the young kids are listening to. He is thirty-six. He buys a U2 record, *War*. The second Christmas my dad tries to come back home. Something goes wrong and he leaves again. It's the saddest day of my childhood. My mother can't get up in the morning, and she stays in bed.

"Take a little green pill, Mom. You'll feel better."

She gives me the money and I buy and wrap the gifts. I'm nine years old.

More, similar Christmases and New Years pass. The recession of '92. My father, a salesman for a big clothing brand, loses his job, I don't really know how. I hear things like "suspension of payments," "crisis in the textile sector in Catalonia," "layoffs," things I've been hearing again lately. For years I don't know exactly what he does, sometimes he represents brands of jeans, or stockings. He carries the samples in a silvery briefcase. My mother, a teacher, supports us on her own.

In his late thirties, my father runs marathons and triathlons – it's that or become an alcoholic, he says. The looks and questions from some of my female teachers when he picks me up at school indicate that he is a seductive man. He starts a relationship with a painter who dyes her hair red. A sophisticated woman who's lived in the capital. She has a daughter four years younger than me. Her parents let them live in an apartment near the center of the city that the family owns and they move in together. The walls are covered in art, loaned by a brother-in-law with a gallery. We play with her many party dresses and her makeup cases. Sometimes I hear them making love and fighting afterward. A record by Juan Luis Guerra often plays. I don't understand why my father now takes another little girl to school.

I express my consternation at not having him at home in a poem, which I write on cardstock made to look like a window, with fabric glued to the top on either side, like curtains. My father hangs it up beside the drawings made by the painter's daughter in the bedroom they share. One day when I get back from school and my father isn't there, she quarrels with me about the poem. My first lesson in the power of the word. Their relationship lasts four years and breaks up after several passionate outbursts. My father still doesn't have a steady job and he doesn't want to show us his new rental apartment on the poor side of town. Years later, his future wife shows me a photo: the apartment is small and sad, its only possession a bicycle. My mother decides to go back to school and isn't home many evenings. The wedding photos still hang on the wall of the dining room. They remain there for many years.

My father's family's version of the separation puts the blame on my mother, a woman obsessed with her work who neglected my father. As for my mother, I soon grow used to being her confidante, to listening time and time again about why they separated (my father's not coming home at night, etc.) like a lesson I failed in school. On both sides they would tell me, both then and later on, to move on, turn the page. So here I am, writing, and turning the page.

Research Notes VI

OCEANOGRAPHY

Yesterday, as I quoted the names of foreign explorers to C, a woman I work with, she told me about Pepita Castellví, the prestigious Catalan oceanographer. I found a speech she gave in 2007, declared International Polar Year, for the inauguration of La Mercè, Barcelona's annual festival:

> [. . .] It is paradoxical that at a time when a large part of humanity has reached a level of scientific and technological development that allows it to tackle challenges beyond Earth, there are parts of this planet that are completely ignored by science. The oceans are the most scandalous example. [. . .] The oceans occupy 75% of the Earth's surface and the underwater reliefs are deeper than those on the surface of the continents. Everest is more than 8,800 meters high, but the deepest sea trench known today is more than 11,000 meters deep. Given these characteristics, it would lead us to think that the most important part of the planet is not the visible land but the large volume of water that surrounds it. [. . .]
>
> At this level the polar regions come into play; their large

masses of ice serve as thermal buffers against the warming waters at lower latitudes. The study of the Antarctic is a new field of study for science. It more or less began in 1957 with the celebration of the Second International Geophysical Year. Spain was left out of that movement, since it was unable and unwilling to take on such a large-scale project at a time when even research on a more accessible scale didn't have the minimum means it needed. [. . .] I like to say that all the events that take place in nature are recorded in the elements, which we have within our reach, like a great big book. The problem is that we don't know how to read what we are being shown. Actually, scientific investigation is nothing more than learning that language in order to be able to interpret what nature is telling us.

[. . .]

I wanted to end with a quote from Ernest Shackleton, the great explorer who led one of the greatest adventures ever in Antarctica: "The Polar Regions leave a profound mark on those who have struggled in them, which is difficult to express to men who have never left the civilized world."

PING-PONG

Sixteen years old. When my mother and I argue, which happens often, I try to go live with my father, whom I adore. His new girlfriend – British, childless, and significantly younger than him – makes an effort to grow into the role, but she wasn't counting on having to live with a teenager. A few days after I settled in on the couch, strange silences and whispering start in their bedroom. I hear a pained voice through the paper-thin walls of the new rental apartment. The next day, the woman sits outside on the balcony and now she's no longer speaking. I grab my rucksack, hop on my second-hand Derbi Variant and go back to my mom's house. Ping-pong. In that period I date a skater quite a bit older than me who lives in a squat. He's twenty-four and his only job, besides skating, is selling hashish. Sometimes I spend the night with him. That's the end of my good grades and awards. I skip school a lot.

Eight years later, my mother still hasn't told anyone at work, or at my school, that she's separated. I imagine that's to avoid pity. At school – an overcrowded public high school in the nineties, one of those prefab barracks that still today are used as patches on the public education system in this country – the students who come from stable environments and aren't very curious do well, other students find opportunities to stray: the local bar, with constant card games and table football, the nearby park, with constant pot smoking. An enthusiastic teacher saves more lives than any of the coppers wandering around those places. It's the art and philosophy professors, not the literature ones, that make me want to stay in class. On my own initiative, I visit the psychologist at the student center. She asks me about the members of my family. She makes some sort of family tree in a file. There are a lot of white spaces. Pieces are missing and the support points are inverted. She looks at me over her glasses, trying to hide her perplexity. She gives me a sheet of paper with a blank schedule. She says I need to get organized. I don't go back.

One day when I go to look at clothes in an alternative-fashion store, the clerk, who has a Mohawk and platform shoes, offers me a job. He says I should go by the club where he works and they'll give me a try. It's the period of the emergence of techno. Laurent Garnier, Jeff Mills, Daft Punk and the best DJs come through that club. After the trial I start working there on the weekends – everybody else is going there too, and that way I can get in free and make some money. I like to dress up and dance.

The guy who hired me, Vanity – he refers to himself in the feminine – also does our makeup, à la *Blade Runner*, Björk, or inspired by anything that seems futuristic, androgynous or Japanese. We wear our hair short and bleached or colorfully dyed, with Mohawks or really long extensions. Because of our proximity to France, that club was one of the first in the country to make the walls tremble to the techno beat. Fueled by Ecstasy, the promise of shared love floats through the place. My favorite wig – which transforms me into a replicant – is purple, very straight and cut into a pageboy. But today I'll wear the silvery geisha one, made out of air-conditioning tubing. In the dressing rooms there are gowns made of colorful, deflated balloons and even stranger, transparent pinafores lined with real candies, some of them missing. Since the wig is eye-catching enough, I choose a short, simple, white number.

The place is booming. Vanity rushes to do our makeup. She paints a horizontal white stripe that covers my eyes and puts on false neon eyelashes.

"Alright, kids, get on down to the dance floor." She claps her hands and lets out a high-pitched giggle.

Outside of the dressing room the decibels are deafening. The club, painted black, is located in a former convent and has three levels: on the top one are the dressing rooms; on the second, a chill-out area with sofas and a small dance floor; on the bottom, the main floor surrounded by various bars, and an outdoor terrace with a swimming pool where most of the regulars have gone swimming in their clothes. Almost six foot one in my white platform boots and white micro-mini dress, I pass through the throng of teenagers, who respond with open smiles and half-maniacal, half-innocent looks of admiration provoked by ecstasy and amphetamines. I leap over the railing on the second floor that separates the foyer from the podium. The DJ welcomes me by slowing down the music's beat and the light technician puts a spotlight on me, changing the color from purple to white. The spotlight blinds me and I feel a comforting warmth. I lift my arms, and look up at the origin of the brightness. The bass in the music vibrates throughout my entire body, there is a suspended moment; Pris, a basic pleasure model of replicant, awakens. Some part of her brain predicts the change in beats perfectly; progression, rising melody line – her arms respond with tai chi movements – five seconds later, climax; boom boom boom boom the bass drum echoes in chest cavities, arms release, her body reacts with the movements of an automaton brought to life. On the dance floor, those with ecstasy in their veins let their eyes half-close and their jaws unhinge. Black light makes their smiles glow and the first chords of the basso continuo in Daft Punk's new song are heard; then comes the vocoder:

Around the world Around the world, Around the world Around the woorld.

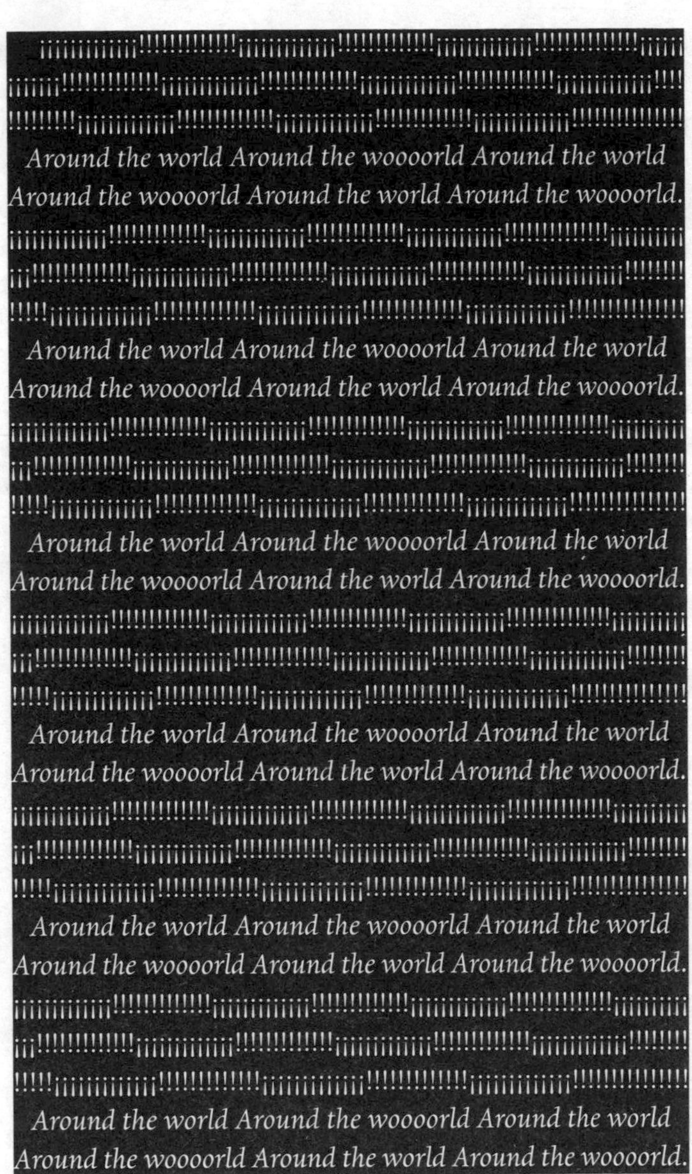
Around the world Around the wooorld Around the world
Around the wooorld Around the world Around the wooorld.
Around the world Around the wooorld Around the world
Around the wooorld Around the world Around the wooorld.
Around the world Around the wooorld Around the world
Around the wooorld Around the world Around the wooorld.
Around the world Around the wooorld Around the world
Around the wooorld Around the world Around the wooorld.
Around the world Around the wooorld Around the world
Around the wooorld Around the world Around the wooorld.
Around the world Around the wooorld Around the world
Around the wooorld Around the world Around the wooorld.

Euphoria. My counterpart appears, a guy with blue hair, his torso nude, metallic pants and white platforms. We transform into mummies, imitating the steps in Michel Gondry's music video. The DJ introduces a new sample. A bruising bass line; everyone shakes their heads, some lift a thumb toward us. The rhythm gets more and more dizzying. The dancing becomes a race. They offer me drinks. I dance out of inertia. They give me a pill. I drink. I hop over the railing and leave the podium to my companion.

It's hard to talk above the music, I can only respond with a slightly forced smile to those who raise their thumbs. Once I get to the dressing rooms I pull the pill out of my pants and toss it into the toilet. At the end of the night, after four shifts of fifteen minutes on the podium, I take off my makeup. Outside, most of the people crowding the front door to the club in varyingly pitiful states are making plans to go to an after-hours spot. Someone says that somewhere on the outskirts of the city there's a rave. The sun comes up. I turn down the offers to join in, and grab my scooter. My mother doesn't allow me to stay out that late, I'll really get it if she catches me. When I get home, frozen, at six-thirty in the morning, I open the door so slowly that the bells tied to the handle don't make a sound. I undress in the apartment's foyer very silently. Ti-ti-ti-ti-ti-ti-ti-ti-ti-ti-ti – an alarm is going off – I quickly hide my clothes in the small studio that is the first door on the right, remaining in panties and a tee shirt. I grab a glass of water from the kitchen. I walk calmly past her bedroom with the glass of water in my hand. The door is ajar, I hear the rustling of sheets.

"That alarm is really annoying, Mom." I feign a sleepy voice.

After a few months I'm tired of the conversations sparked by a round of shots, I realize that I'm spending most of what I earn keeping up that lifestyle. One day, I just don't go back.

Reading is my favorite subversive activity, which I don't identify with the stuffy literature classes taught by ladies who seem like they must have been born fifty years old. *Fortunata and Jacinta*, Benito Pérez Galdós, the Generation of '98. Yuck. I skip class to go read in the bar near my high school; I visit Henry Miller's *Tropics*, I am Anaïs Nin's confidante. Reading is an alienating activity that's more fun, more socially accepted, and cheaper than drugs. I read without any criteria: new releases, romantic paperbacks by Corín Tellado, psychology, philosophy and pedagogy text books that I find around the house, inherited from my aunt, a professor who left us some boxes of books when she moved. My favorite title is *How to Philosophize with a Hammer*, by some dude named Nietzsche. Its contents are incomprehensible but fascinating to me. N-I-T-X . . .

Sha-kes-pe-ar-e.

Prust.

Research Notes VII

A CALL FROM THE ARCTIC

My father set up a treadmill a neighbor gave him in my bedroom at my mom's house, so my brother would get some exercise. The room is small and filled with dressers. It has a window that opens onto the inner courtyard, where we hang up our clothes to dry. I rarely sleep there, but it is important for me to know that there's some stable place where I can leave my books and whatever's left over from a move, and come back for them at some other time. An anchoring point. Having that small room completely filled with a machine more suited to a villa than an apartment bugs me. And my brother never uses it anyway. I think about calling someone instead of staying at home writing. My father is celebrating Christmas with his other family, visiting Santa Claus in Lapland. Evenings, when you have no plans to see anyone later, can be menacing. I let my boyfriend go away for the weekend with some friends. It's not the first time. The little time I have to write is precious to me.

"You stay and do your artist stuff," he said through clenched teeth before leaving.

Doubt and loneliness are persistent. I don't know if writing all this is worth the effort, or whether I have any right.

"Worse / Even than your maddening / Song, your silence," Sylvia Plath reminds me.

I think about calling someone, but all my friends are away for the holidays. My mother, twenty years a single, met someone a few months ago on a dating site, and she seems happy. Her calls come less frequently. I tell myself that an hour of exercise will wipe it all away. For some of us, Christmas is a regression to our teenage years.

Soon I'll be back to my work routine. Then I won't think about all that. But I'll return to it occasionally: on holidays, on some weekend alone. Just when I'm about to shut down my computer, I get a rare call from my father. He tells me what his Christmas at the Arctic Circle is like. Sometimes I think we maintain a certain telepathy – which we had when I was a girl. Did he hear that I was thinking of him? He tells me about visiting Santa Claus with his wife's nieces and nephews, the igloo hotels, and the tours in sleighs drawn by reindeer. It's all really touristy, he says. I don't get the chance to ask him about the aurora borealis because we get cut off. I don't have a lot of coverage in the studio. I call it the igloo.

M

I'd have to go back one more generation to properly contextualize my parents (we really should go back a couple of generations to understand any of us), including why I have no grandmothers and only one grandfather when the other is still alive. Then there's this thing with my brother, which no one knows the cause of. I don't know if I can explain that story now. I don't even know it myself.

I have the feeling that my life began when M was born, seven years before me. My appearance was unplanned. When my mother found out she was pregnant, she cried. Later – she told me twenty years afterward – she thought that M would need a sister.

There was risk of a miscarriage at first. It seems that with that warning, the doctor ordered my parents to be very careful and my mother, naturally active and energetic, was confined to bed. The pregnancy went on almost ten months, since in the end I didn't want to come out – both my premature leaving home and my reluctance to leave the womb are typical of me, and probably understandable.

A few days before they were going to induce labor, on January 5, 1982, the eve of Epiphany, the streets invaded by royal carriage floats with the three kings' pages tossing candy to the children, I showed up.

My mother says that I was born with my eyes open, and that I was looking at her.

DECEMBER 27, 2013

News item:

Luminous night-time clouds in the Antarctic

Data received from NASA's AIM satellite shows that the luminous blue clouds that appear each austral summer over Antarctica are like large "geophysical lightbulbs." They return each year as spring ends, and they are at their full intensity for no longer than five to ten days. As the month of December continues, a large bank of luminous clouds stops over Antarctica. It began this year on November 20 as a small electric blue cloud and quickly expanded to cover almost the entire continent. AIM is monitoring the clouds' progress as they swirl and wave around the South Pole. "The clouds appeared over the South Pole earlier than usual this year," says Cora Randall from Colorado's Laboratory for Atmospheric and Space Physics, a member of the AIM's scientific team. "Since AIM has been in orbit, the only earlier start was in the 2009 season," she said. The luminous clouds are the highest ones on the planet. Sown with disintegrating meteoroids, they form on the edge of space 83 kilometers above the Earth's surface. When light hits the tiny ice crystals that make up these clouds, they seem to glow with an intense, electric-blue tone. These blue clouds are most widespread and brightest during the austral summer. They light up over the South Pole from November to February, and move to the North Pole for May to August.[7]

[7] http://www.lavanguardia.com/vida/20131227/54397579936/aparecen-nubes-azules-sobre-antartida.html.

LEAVING HOME

The last year of high school I focus on studying; my motivation is the desire to escape to the capital. My mother asks me if my chosen major will allow me to teach, I answer in the affirmative and she lets me go. I do decently on the university entrance exam and enter Fine Arts. In the early days of the twenty-first century, the Fine Arts building, tucked behind the Architecture Faculty, is a terrarium of strange species where the professors occasionally stick their heads in to see what's going on. The Philosophy and Art History libraries stick out like temples above a Martian colony in the nearly barren wasteland where transvestites and transsexuals make their rounds in the evening, sometimes sharing the faculty bar. The libraries will be my home for the next few years.

After two years at school, my father's work situation improves, and I don't have to work at the clothing store on weekends and holidays. I'm twenty years old and I think I can start fresh when and where it strikes my fancy. That summer I go to London to learn English with a travel grant from the Ministry of Education. On the lawn of Regent's Park and reading *A Room of One's Own* by Virginia Woolf, I realize what conquering that room of my own – where I'd never yet written – will cost me. Searching for housing on a message board at the university where I'm studying, I meet S, a law student. His house has quite a few books and films and I decide to take the room. It's the largest one I've ever had, with a window that looks out onto a garden in Camden Town. The brick house is nothing special by British standards. For me, it is paradise. Close to Primrose Hill, where a few years later Amy Winehouse would live. I fantasize about staying, but London is insanely expensive. The guy flatters me with gifts and starts to control me. Since the grant isn't very generous and I don't want to return home in debt, I take a job in a neighborhood shoe store to pay for the extra costs of the trip. I swap intellectual discussions on campus lawns for the store basement, for checking inventory, piles of unmatched shoes, and meetings to applaud the "salesperson of the week." Each of our sales figures is ranked on the staff-room door and there are arguments over commissions when more than one person helped a customer. I have to go back and finish my last year of school. I get home in late August, relieved. After a few distant months, my friendship with S lasts many years. In Barcelona I return to the icy austerity of a shared student apartment in Collblanc, the border between Les Corts and L'Hospitalet. Despite having a relatively clean space, I don't find the camaraderie I was imagining between four students from the sticks. I keep looking for an apartment – even now I'm still in the habit of looking at every bulletin board, even now that they've migrated to the internet. Anxiety and guilt over studying something that doesn't promise a clear future. After studying the arts, many classmates will end up working as waiters and museum guards – jobs that seem to emerge as the only solution. I spend my days at the library, drawing, or practicing different techniques. I read a lot and don't make many friends. I discover Proust. I imagine a middle-class woman trying to be Proust. How can you tell a story with that depth without the necessary time that a trust fund brings? Is wanting to be an artist and writer suicide? Common sense drops like a ton of bricks on these questions.

The first years at university I discover conceptual art, even though it seems like something I can't yet allow myself. I devote myself to learning how to paint, confusing technique with art. After all, when you are very young and have little to say, you can do one of two things: speak from your heart, which runs the risk of saying what thousands of people have said better before you, or focus on your references, mediums, and forms. In my case I'd already acquired prejudices about artistic techniques, so I chose the latter. I work in different styles at the same time, from the geometric abstraction of American painting in the fifties to the realism of British painting in the eighties, inspired by Lucian Freud. What I'm doing isn't "fresh," or conceptual, or interesting from a technical perspective, the three prevailing trends. But I don't allow myself to play; my clearest insights remain in my notebooks, as quick sketches, brief texts, and poems. Only later will I learn to recognize that material. More than anything else, those are years of learning the necessary discipline to create a project from zero, and finish it.

I'm worried about creating things that only the upper class will be able to buy, and in most cases will leave those of us who produce them in a precarious financial state. We need to have a voice and it has to reach the right audience. Finding it is a much more costly path than the technical training, since it is so much about recognizing your own identity.

Soon I become interested in creating artists' books, a more accessible and reproducible format than paintings, to which I can also add text. Writing still seems like a privilege I haven't earned and one I was denied during my high school years. My study habits are weak and all the classes I skipped show. We wrote little, and apart from editing for spelling and grammar, they didn't give us much advice on style or structure. It takes me a couple of years to make the dean's list in theoretical subjects.

The book as object stops being of interest to me. I start anew, switching to Literature despite the skeptical comments of some of my classmates and the opposition of my family; there is a certain amount of prejudice against "the artist" as someone who cannot or should not adapt to conventional environments. Years later I think that it was the best decision I could take. As for the costs associated with it, now that my father is doing well, I ask him to help me to continue paying for the room in the shared apartment while I study. He is about to get married and buy a house. He accepts begrudgingly. He sends over money for the room and spaces out his calls. I take care of paying for the tuition and other expenses. My decision to study Literary Theory, which slows my path to economic independence and lengthens my material hardships, costs me a cold – and sometimes less cold – war with my paternal family, who feels he's helped me enough. Other motives converge to create a prolonged campaign of exclusion from my father's side of the family, motives that would unnecessarily extend this narration with explanations more or less justifiable if this were my own defense in a trial. I'm trying to allude to the complex sentimental origins of the conflict, which the reader, more attentive to the omissions – amid the snow – than what is explained, can interpret according to their perspective and intuition.

Simultaneously I work as a cultural guide; I repeat six times a day, three days a week, in English, Catalan, and Spanish, the wonders of the Palau de la Música to an audience of fifty-five people. It ends up being a crash course in oratory, diction, and interpretation. I'm pretty good at it, judging by the tips I receive from the tourists. That is right before the scandal breaks over the management of that historical building by the Millet family; the Palau is a huge cash register that alternates all sorts of concerts – of dubious artistic selection and criteria – with guided tours every fifteen minutes. The groups of amazed tourists even interrupt rehearsals, silencing the orchestra. More than €8,000 a day comes in from visits, not including the profits from the concerts. This is 2008, the year the real estate bubble bursts. It is impossible to find another job. After two years, having explained the interior of the Palau de la Música more than a thousand times and about to go mad from an overdose of Catalan Art Nouveau, I finally find a part-time job as a teacher.

Considering the subject and the state of secondary education in this country, teaching teenagers in the early evening kills off the few artistic airs I still had. Even when you are very young, teaching high school leads the people around you to assume that your artistic pretensions have gone up in smoke, and if you are a writer, you will soon quit. Perhaps that was a lesson in humility. Vanity, what little I still had then out of pure ignorance, is something that radiates out and stops you from seeing what's in front of you. Like sadness or excessive introspection, two birds that sometimes pursue me and which I try to shoo away, even though writing in and of itself isn't always the best antidote for them.

THE GIFTS

C and R are *tuning-fork friends*; they give the pitch for your voice. Tuning-fork people are intelligent (highly intelligent, although that isn't essential), and above all it's important that they be good. These are the type of people you need to bounce things off of. Amid giggles, we tell each other about the various misunderstandings and arguments with our partners over Christmas presents. In the end we are discussing the areas of conflict that arise when those romantic and economic currents intersect. The subject speaks volumes about the place we give to relationships, and particularly about the expectations, visions of the other person, and reciprocity in play. I remember having heard *Essai sur le don* (*The Gift*) by Marcel Mauss, a professor of anthropology, mentioned in this regard. Even though Mauss studied archaic societies, he said what we all know and understand: that giving an object (gift) enhances the giver and creates an inherent obligation in the receiver to reciprocate. I've heard a friend say the opposite, that accepting a gift honors the recipient: "I accept this gift, therefore I allow you to give it." This point accentuates the fact that it is the recipient who has the last word, so their role is not passive. Even still, accepting gifts is not voluntary, but rather almost obligatory: refusing them creates conflicts. The way things have been in these recent years of recession, many of us found ourselves obligated to accept monetary gifts from family members once we were past the "official" age for receiving them. Perhaps the relative gave the gift with the best of intentions, and the only thing they wanted to do was help. But sometimes a condescending smile is involved, and the gift becomes charity.

Giving something creates a bridge, a connection that is somewhat unstable, perhaps in the hopes of things balancing out in the future, or to compensate a past situation deemed "excessive" or generous on the other's part, and not necessarily in a material sense. We sometimes want to give someone something because their presence and their friendship are or could become important to us, but without expecting any reciprocal gift. At Christmas, you can find justifications for the act of "giving" that are about the children's happiness and about expressing love in the immediate family. Out of a pure spirit of contradiction I entertain thoughts of negative variations on the gift:

Poisoned Gift: it creates a much larger or more valuable obligation than the cost of the gift. When it is accepted, it highlights the fact that the receiver is accepting it for some reason (see *bribe*).

The well-known *Regift*: a useless, ugly thing that we've been gifted and we put back into circulation with relief and some fear of being found out. The most perverse thing about regifting is that the second giving transforms the initial giver's good intentions into sarcasm.

Betrayal Gift: a particularly flattering portrait made by our partner at a high point in the relationship, or a dress given by a lover, that is used after the breakup as an instrument in the search (on- or offline) for a new partner.

Apology Gift: I'll give you something so I don't have to ask for forgiveness.

Gift for Me (which is different than a *Gift to Myself*): that's when I give you something because it's in my best interests: X gives a television to Y, who doesn't have one. (X likes to watch TV and wants to be able to when he visits Y.) The list is long, since gifts to others are often gifts for ourselves. That ties in to the next type:

Greed: go shopping for gifts and only find gifts you give to yourself.

Potlatch Gift: competitive giving between various members of a family or group. In this case the most expensive gift can create a conflict with the receiver, for not having corresponded in the same measure. This rarely happens among young people or families of meager means, but close sources assure us that these rivalries exist.

No Gift: we said we don't want a gift, but we really do (maybe we don't want to be asked what we want). The giver takes us at our word. Here you get what you ask for.

Crap Gift/Gift Crap: "Some gifts come wrapped in shit," says a friend about a failed relationship and the revelation he had when leaving it behind. "Some gifts can turn out to be shit," I think about a relationship and the trauma left in its wake.

The underlying question is: at what point does the verb *to give* intersect with the verb *to be*, in other words, what is it about "you" that is "given"? Because a relationship always involves this transit between one and the other, this coming and going that objects sometimes embody.

STALKER

I run into Iceberg at a concert. Or more precisely, he runs into me. When he greets me he's unusually cordial. I'd be lying if I said I never google him. After an argument with your partner you can always find an ocean of information to wallow in: Twitter, Facebook, articles, images, and of course their blog, if they have one. I'm with two girlfriends. The concert starts and they pull me toward the front. I tell them I'll catch up in a minute. Considering the chances of my getting lost in the crowd, I just showed excessive interest. Once we've covered our usual shared topics, I bring up The Topic – How's your thesis going? My thesis is frozen and on the verge of shipwreck. I manage to seem stupidly interested in his stuff. I am stupidly interested in his stuff. The next day the question of whether or not to add him on the social networks gnaws at me. I could have done it before, made a friend request, like other classmates have, but he hasn't shown any signs of friendship since we were in school together. Despite that, he was the one who came over to me, I tell myself, again stupidly. I could add him. Maybe that way – bringing him into my day-to-day – I'll stop idealizing him.

The next day I send him a friend request and he accepts immediately. Since I took the first step, I wait for some sign of connection, some gesture of support, or a like on something I've posted. After a while, and since we have some shared literary predilections, I give him a like. The stone doesn't even graze the window. It's followed by various posts with good news about my stuff. Nothing. Followed by various bits of good news about his stuff. Me: like. Him: zip. Me: 0, Him: 1. I always come out losing with numbers. Iceberg rarely gives a like to any of our mutual friends. It must be because he's stingy and egocentric. Or because he goes into Facebook to post about his things but doesn't pay attention to the rest, which probably corroborates my first supposition. As for me, after a few months it's clear that he doesn't even have any interest in maintaining a cordial relationship. My category in his value scale is *follower*.

My father sometimes compares people to cars or shoes. And his advice is in step: "They shouldn't hurt when you walk." The metaphor of friction when walking is pretty graphic, but the comparison person/product, particularly with a shoe, is denigrating. As I think about it more, I realize that I've had shoes that hurt at first but later were my most comfortable pair. When I could still talk to him about these things, and I mentioned something about it, he said Iceberg seemed like the Ferrari type. The person/car comparison seems a bit less humiliating than the shoe one but this time blatantly classist. His tone when he says "a Ferrari" is: *too-dear-for-you.* I mutate from young woman to utilitarian car, from utilitarian car to house slipper. I can't come up with any consoling or dignifying referent for that situation. The first image that comes to my mind is male, and it's that cinematic losers – to avoid beating a dead (female) horse – have always been men. I could be a charming loser like Jack Lemmon in *The Apartment.*

Letter from an Unknown Woman is the only literary work about unrequited female love that I can think of right now. The problem is that, as often happens in novels of that period, she has to die in the end, and I'd like to reserve the right to a less dramatic ending, or – if I can dream – a triumphant one. The character is a servant who sends flowers every year to a young, talented writer, who has no idea who is sending them. "I speak only to you; for the first time I will tell you everything, the whole story of my life, a life that has always been yours although you never knew it. But you shall know my secret only once I am dead, when you no longer have to answer me, when whatever is now sending hot and cold shudders through me really is the end."[8] I read Zweig's original in German class. Trying to sum up the book, while searching for justifications for both characters' behavior – for her obsession, for his cluelessness – another student was more concise: He's an imbecile. Moral interpretations are always reassuring. The fundamental question is as simple as a song by Beyoncé: Why don't you love me?

The internet and our own marketing of our personalities, all of us converted into *followers* and *followed* (lovers and beloveds), stars and stalkers at the same time.

[8] Translation by Anthea Bell.

THE COLDEST PLACE

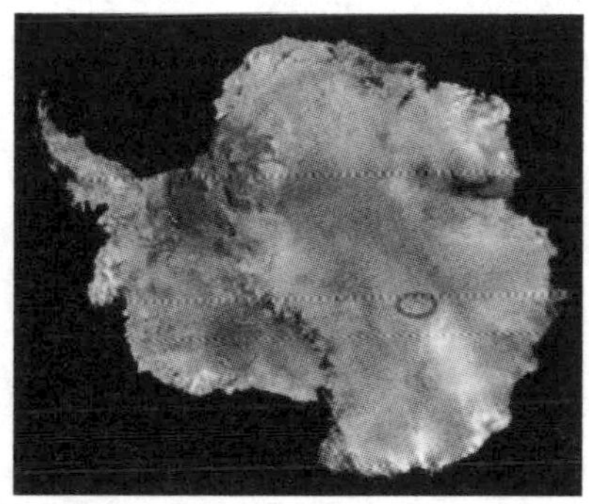

DECEMBER 10, 2013

The white continent has broken the absolute record of lowest recorded temperature: -93.2°C, on August 10, 2010. This is the result of the analysis of the most detailed temperature maps of the Earth to date and based on 32 years' worth of data taken by satellites.[9]

[9] http://sociedad.elpais.com/sociedad/2013/12/10/actualidad/1386692048_411194.html.

The Antarctic image, with its cold blue stripe in the center, reminds me of a heart:

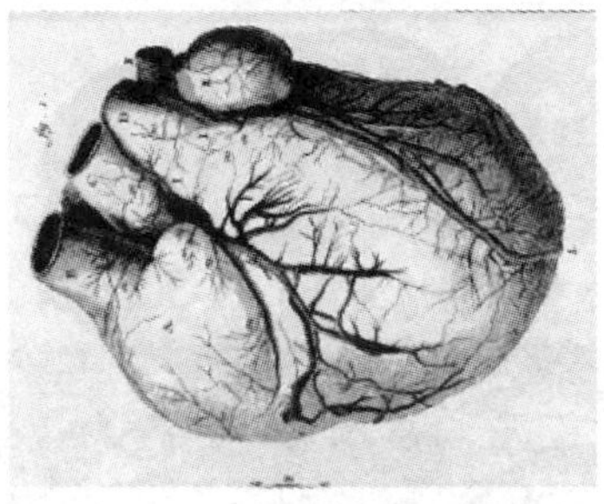

-93.2°C

IN FRONT OF YOU

Writing is not inside you, it's in front of you, says Casanova in *Story of My Death*, the film by Albert Serra. A statement that can lead us in two directions: writing as a dialogue with the world rather than a tool for introspection, or in a second sense, which doesn't contradict the first, writing as pure form materialized in the text, mere language. As if that Casanova, collector of intimacies, were reminding us that there is nothing intimate about writing. In the film, one character turns shit into gold, another worships his shit. And that suggests an underlying truth: we are alchemists; like worms, we secrete silk. Our presence in crumbling urban areas gives them new prestige, we convert thwarted loves into songs, artistic installations denouncing the evictions caused by the recession will end up being bought for the collection of a multinational investment bank. Sublimators, now instrumentalized, workers at the symbolic sewage treatment plant.

While transforming happiness, beauty, and seduction into gold doesn't cost much (the alchemical process is equivalent to a simple change of mold), converting shit into gold is a costly process both for the organism who undertakes it and, indirectly, for its environment. In many cases it can cost years of solitude and/or accusations of egotism from their family. On top of facing the incomprehension caused when someone chooses periods of solitary work, even though they are already carrying out a productive task that satisfies their material needs, there is the anxiety generated by that very job, which is often just something to put food on the table and in no way a realization of their calling. This feeling that ranges from anxiety to slight unease can, at the same time, feed the alchemical process, which is carried out in parallel, discreetly when not furtively, because even if the Author – from this point on: the worm – wanted to reveal the inner processes that are consuming him or her, no one could fully understand them. Taken to an extreme, this compulsion and need for isolation can generate accusations that lead to expulsion from the family. Once, even, due to an insatiable writing compulsion, a worm turned into a beetle. As for this author, the process can be intermittently accompanied by an absorbing monologue that only finds its way out in front of a keyboard; the monologue could last days, or months, or years, with varying degrees of intensity, until the resolution or exhaustion of the conflict that gave rise to it (vulgarly and not coincidentally called shit). Often it is fueled by a glimpse of a way out in real life, which will have to be resolved in life and not through the digestive process, yet that process will be part and parcel of the conflict's resolution.

The period of time needed to transfigure shit into gold, a process that can only be done by a certain species of worm, depends on the obligations and material needs that worm has, just like most other larvae and insects. The time varies according to the responsibilities that force it to postpone its digestive processes for months. During that time the worm can maintain contact with what is cooking inside it through maintaining enough reading and quick note-taking to keep the process latent. In more intensive work periods, necessary for the deep elaboration and final expulsion of that which must come out, this worm will notice the progressive shrinking of the diameter of its hair, which will thin out as the months pass until a long period of calm, of no digestion, re-establishes its normal thickness. In intensive phases when the worm is elaborating some sort of transformation of grief, the trash bin will daily ingest chunks of hair as big as fists, that appear in the comb of this vertebrate worm. As time passes, new hair will slowly appear on its scalp, sometimes changing its hair type; from wavy to straight, or from straight to wavy, so slowly that no one else will notice it. The effects of the transformation are similar to those of a hormonal change. In parallel the worm could lose – has lost – between five and ten kilos of body mass: the sublimation process involved in converting shit into gold is not free; it is a dangerous and expensive process for the small larval organism, which could collapse if what it tries to digest is too large for its digestive track. There are remains, shit, conflicts that are too severe to process; a large amount of human evil is indigestible for this worm, who is aware that they would saturate the defenses of its small organism, capable only of digesting conflicts on a local scale. The worm, whose process you can witness on these pages, hopes in the future to secrete lighter constructions. For the time being, its trail, the trail of its costly headway, is in front of you.

THE BASEMENT

Sick and tired of acting out a dialogue with myself, I decide to seek out an interlocutor. A friend recommends one. His office is uptown, in a discreet location. A silver plaque states his name beneath the intercom "TD, Psychologist – Psychoanalyst." I see a tall man arrive, wearing a motorcycle helmet and with a briefcase in one hand. I imagine that it's him. After a little while, I ring the bell again. This time I'm buzzed in. The office is in the basement of an old, well-maintained building. I go down the dim stairs to the office. I'm received by a man younger than I was expecting, dark with fine features, his head completely shaved in a way that underscored, rather than hid, his premature balding. I can't place his accent, which is from somewhere in South America, but not Argentina, which is what you'd expect according to cliché. The basement is an apartment with modern detailing. There are African masks on the wall. There is a loft space with a large library filled with wooden shelves curving under the weight of the books. The windows touch the ceiling, little light comes in. We shake hands and he asks me to take a seat.

"Very well. What brings you here?"

". . ."

"How could you tell that that bothered your father's family, how could they see in you the chance to unload?"

". . ."

"Somehow, not saying anything, has to do with accepting it. You can realize that in the face of an attack, not only would your father not be on your side, but you'd be subject to a new attack . . . How vulnerable might you feel at that moment?"

". . ."

(I grab the first tissue.)

"So in order for one to be part of the family, acceptance is necessary."

". . ."

"Regrettably, they aren't here. We are going to focus on you, on what position you can occupy."

"?"

"One that concerns the answer."

". . ."

"But why represent that position of inevitable family friction? That position seems key."

". . ."

"Perhaps before you weren't in the situation, now you are. And in any case, that position isn't an inevitable place. One can choose the responsibilities one wants to take on."

". . ."

"That position isn't coincidental. From it we can identify it, no, shift it, or question these perspectives."

POLAR VORTEX

TUESDAY, JANUARY 7, 2013

News item:

New York freezes, recording the lowest temperature in 118 years.

> All eyes are on the thermometer. The states of Pennsylvania, New York and New Jersey are between -15 and -18°C; -22°C in the city of Chicago (Illinois) and -16°C in the capital, Washington D.C. The wave of polar cold affecting half of the United States has broken temperature records in numerous regions, even hitting southern cities such as Atlanta (Georgia) and Birmingham (Alabama) where -6°C is expected. Americans have become familiar with the meteorological term "polar vortex," which is the name for the cyclone that has come down from the pole to freeze a swath of the country from the Rocky Mountains all the way to the East Coast. At Dulles International Airport, in Washington D.C., temperatures have dipped lower than the 1996 record of -13°C, before causing the

gauges to fail, according to a report from the National Weather Service.[10]

New York frozen, Niagara Falls frozen.

[10] http://internacional.elpais.com/internacional/2014/01/07/actualidad/1389114377_203636.html.

STAGNATION, FREEZING, RUPTURE

After a few apathetic weekends, E and I decide to end our relationship. I'm scared to give up the emotional stability, affection, and companionship, but I can't be with someone while I'm thinking about someone else, even someone fictional. Maybe I've invented him in order to write this book.

I work long hours on freelance jobs in addition to teaching, and I look for an apartment.

I lose a few kilos. It's February and a cold wind is blowing.

FEBRUARY

During my move out of the apartment I've shared for the last three years, I find a newspaper clipping that a friend – who knows about my Arctic obsessions – left on the desk in my studio. The feature story on some photographs from Shackleton's expedition recently found under the ice is a couple of pages long and dated January 5, my birthday.

> The recent finding of twenty-two negatives in a small box in the darkroom at the cabin in Cape Evans, which was the

> main base for Scott's 1911 expedition, allows us another look at the heroic period of polar exploration and invites us to reflect on the important role of photography in those episodes of grand characters, feats and disasters. [. . .] Two of the photos rescued and painstakingly restored by the Antarctic Heritage Trust, the New Zealand organization charged with conserving various historic places in the Ross Sea region, show Alexander Stevens, a member of the Imperial Trans-Antarctic Expedition (1914–1917), the famous voyage led by Ernest Shackleton with the aim of crossing the continent. Its failure gave rise to what is considered one of the most extraordinary adventures of endurance, courage, and leadership in the history of exploration.[11]

In the article, the author uses the find to review the most emblematic photographs in the history of Antarctica, mentioning their creators: heroic Frank Hurley for the photos of Shackleton's expedition, Herbert Ponting, who documented Scott's expedition. He also mentions the famous photograph – the one I find the most unsettling and evocative – of the conquest of the South Pole by the Norwegian Roald Amundsen. The photo was taken by Olav Bjaaland and shows Amundsen and his three companions with their heads bare (at -23°C) looking at the small tent they've put up, crowned with their country's flag. Around them, there is nothing.

[11] http://sociedad.elpais.com/sociedad/2014/01/04/actualidad/1388867097_208652.html.

> How does anyone portray for posterity the conquest of a place that is an absolutely empty geographic abstraction? 2,594 km and 99 days of expedition require having some idea about how to tackle the visual documentation of the feat. "Back at home everyone was waiting to see the photo of the South Pole, the great trophy, but [italics mine] *how does anyone make the invisible visible?* There was nothing there to show," declares the scholar of the history of the explorations Harald Østgaard Lund, the curator of a large photographic exhibit on the Norwegian polar heroes in Oslo. "They finally managed to create that photo that is etched into the Norwegian collective memory. Converting the South Pole into a real place. Basically, all the explorers used the same idea of a mound, a tent, and a flag."

How to make the invisible visible is a rare question for explorers, and a very common one for artists. An entire nation asking itself this question is a landmark in art. The extremes under which that image was created – the extremes of land, effort, climate, and of all that is (in)visible, white – underscore the profoundly fictitious nature of the document: the gesture and the landscape are pure staging. They could have been found in the snowy garden of someone's house. And therein lies the fascination I feel for that image. It documents pure abstraction, a place triply invisible – an extreme geographic point based on a calculation; and something else that doesn't exist: the conquest of a shifting point; and all this on a white backdrop, invisible from the photographic perspective. The ability to synthesize these various layers of abstraction on a single level is the essence of *making the invisible visible*. Isn't that conquest? Isn't that Art? Three friends playing in the snowy garden.

APRIL

It's spring and this year I have money. I have a new apartment, unfurnished, just for me. A renovated apartment, with appliances and a parquet floor. Working more has its rewards, even though now I don't have time for my polar obsessions. During Easter Week most of my friends are traveling with their significant others. I don't want to spend the week alone and shuttered up in the house; I download an application and after a couple of days of chatting, I meet up with some guy, B, at the bar where my neighbor F is DJing. He's late. In the meantime F introduces me to R, another friend of hers. B arrives an hour later and R has already asked for my number. B notices something odd about the situation. For a moment, they wait, one in front of the other – they both are about the same height, around six foot one, brown hair, beards. Somewhat disconcerted, they switch stools; R gives up his, which is closer to me, and leaves perplexed. The conversation with B bores me. Two days later, I delete my profile.

R

Dark. Prominent nose with soft angles. Wide forehead with slightly receding hairline. Trim, well-shaped beard. Small, penetrating, dark eyes, prone to laughter. A small mouth with thick lips, regular teeth, with particularly pointy canines. A taller and somewhat wider body than average. It's hard to tell whether he's the wolf or the woodcutter. The day after his crestfallen departure from the bar, I send him a friend request on Facebook. The following day he suggests we go to a jazz concert and dinner. At the concert, his physical presence surrounds me in a special way. During dinner he tells me about his parents' divorce. It seems a little early for such subjects but I don't overthink it. He walks me to my old scooter. One of the last gifts from my father during a period of ceasefire, that my students often make fun of. He says goodbye with a quick hug, one of those American-style hugs that lack both the formality of a kiss on each cheek and the warmth of a real hug, and he leaves.

When I get home I send him a message:

"Did the scooter scare you off?" I jest, referring to his defeated air.

"Haha, no . . . Lately I've been kinda tired. I really enjoyed our dinner, when can we do it again?"

We make plans for that same week. Then come the kisses, the flowers, the dinners at restaurants, and the dinners at home.

NORTHWARD

R introduces me to his friend N. A thirty-four-year-old German woman living in Berlin. She represents indie music groups. She's organized tours for bands like Arcade Fire and Death Cab for Cutie. She went through a breakup a year ago. The dinner conversation: What city should we live in? N travels a lot, works online and can live wherever she wants. Copenhagen, Oslo, Helsinki . . .

"I'm looking for a place to live," she tells me.

Like all Germans, N isn't afraid to get deep quickly; we have a long conversation ahead of us. I tell her that sometimes you have to stay, stay and fight, because leaving can be running away, full flight forward.

A couple of days later I meet up with M, my roommate for over five years. First we lived in a tiny apartment on a very narrow street in the old city, later in Gràcia. M is back from a couple of years in Berlin. The company she worked for – a TV channel devoted to video art – has folded. She broke up with her long-term boyfriend in Germany. She takes refuge at her parent's house. She thinks about leaving again. Maybe London. She has little savings. Thirty-five years old. The months pass. We talk about Brussels, London, Reykjavík . . . The answer is always further north.

JULY

Comparing the Amundsen and Scott expeditions on Wikipedia, it appears the main strategic difference is that Amundsen used sleds with dogs from Greenland for his transport, while Scott used Mongolian ponies. Amundsen decided to sacrifice several dogs before reaching the pole and store the meat for the return trip; this strategy allowed him to reduce the burden of dog food and ensure he could maintain the surviving animals on the way back. Scott's ponies had to carry sacks of oats for their feed, which increased their burden and the chances of them sinking into the snow. Another disadvantage was that the ponies' sweat froze on their coats, while the dogs regulated their temperature by panting.

It seems that Amundsen's expedition had better equipment, and clothing that was more resistant to the cold. All of Scott's ponies died and the team had to go it alone. Scott added an extra team member at the last minute, which strained the food-rationing plan. While Amundsen's voyage was efficient and suffered no serious setbacks, Scott reached the pole after great hardships, found Amundsen's tent marking the Norwegian victory, and after documenting his defeat in the famous photograph, he and his entire team died on the return trip.

OCTOBER 21, 2014
LETTER FROM THE ANTARCTIC

The ice rarely releases its grip on the polar explorers it captures – the frozen corpses of Captain Scott and his ill-fated team are still there somewhere flowing slowly along with the Antarctic continental drift – but sometimes it gives back some of their possessions, which is always thrilling. That is the case with a notebook, recently found in the old base at Cape Evans, which belonged to George Murray Levick (1876–1956), one of the sixty-five members of the 1910–1913 *Terra Nova* expedition. While Scott was attempting to reach the South Pole:

> Murray Levick was spending the austral summer of 1911–1912 in the midst of an Adélie penguin rookery. He is still the only person to have spent an entire breeding cycle there. His notes about the penguins' sexual habits, which included sexual coercion, sex among males and sex with dead females, were deemed too indecent for publication at the time, so he wrote them in Greek, so that only an educated gentleman would be able to read them.[12]

[12] https://en.wikipedia.org/wiki/George_Murray_Levick.

I recover my notebook, also frozen for a few months. The ice reminded me of my brother. I call my mother. She's tired, as usual. I asked her about him. She told me that he's been doing well since he found a girlfriend at the day center. At midday they give them some time alone, and they hold hands (she is in a wheelchair).

I ask her about her boyfriend.

"Good, I'm happy. The other day we were kissing and I asked your brother if it bothered him. He answered, 'No, I've got my own now.'"

When I visit them the weekend after that, my mother shows me a letter:

> Dear M,
>
> i love you all infinite eternity and i'll never grow tired of you.
>
> Iloveyou Iwantyou
>
> [drawings of pink hearts and a red heart run through with an arrow]
>
> AB

F

When I found the apartment the first thing I did was get in touch with F. I knew she lived nearby. We had mutual friends and we often saw each other at concerts. Maybe because she was blond, intelligent, and not terribly lucky with guys, the concept *femme fatale* could come to mind as a first impression. It's an expression I've always thought must have been invented by a scared man (or more precisely a scared Hollywood).

F DJs on Fridays at a bar in the old city. That was where I met R who, since he was alone, also came by to visit her.

F represents some local bands, which, as is often the case, doesn't give her enough to live on, so she rents out her house on Airbnb. When someone was staying there she would come sleep at my place, and maybe because I've never had a sister, her company and familiarity, even though it was brought about by the necessity of circumstance, felt good. F is very talkative; she puts it all out there. Maybe it's because she found her mother dead from a combination of pills and alcohol when she was sixteen years old. And since her father left home when she was a baby, she was left basically alone. Well, alone with her grandmother. F is one of those people who seem to have no trouble asking for help when they need it; it's as if she expanded the function of one mother into various people; she has a wide network of friends she can go to when she needs advice or simply someone to listen. F is some sort of centrifugal hurricane. Otherwise, she told me, she would have jumped out a window. Maybe her mother's death, looking on the bright side, was lucky in a way: her mother was perpetually trying to pass the exam to become a public prosecutor, and had the same plans for her daughter.

Once I spent the night at her family house in a small town. I slept in a room that that seemed like it hadn't been used in a long time, filled with furniture from the seventies and old portraits of girls. One of them was her mother as a child. The next morning her grandmother appeared in an elegant black robe, cinched around her thin eighty-six-year-old body. She had an angular face with big blue eyes and a slight tan. Her blond hair was perfectly coiffed and sprayed in place. In one hand she held a very thin cigarette. It almost looked like she was going to a party, except it was ten in the morning on a Saturday, and she was wearing a house robe, not a dress. She looked at me with the expression of a skittish cat. I mentioned that she resembled her granddaughter and it seemed she tried on a smile. Sometimes in families there are particularly strong, charismatic, or luminous characters. Those characters, if they are too focused on themselves, sometimes leave victims around them. Or perhaps it's adverse climates that cause these extreme survival strategies and personalities.

F spends those days when she's rented out her apartment between her grandmother's house and various friends' places, including mine. That's when F shows up with her little pink backpack. She's never liked the idea of growing up. Because as a girl her mother would tell her that they couldn't pay the bills, because she knew that her father drank, and she saw that her mother drank. So the idea of growing up – this came out over more than a decade of therapy – scares her. F shows up at my place with her "little backpack," her headband, and her sparkly sneakers.

"Can I use your shower? I like your shampoos better than D's."

She goes into the bathroom, puts her favorite program on the radio. She doesn't come out for a good long while.

SEARCHING FOR AN ANSWER WHEN THE UNCERTAINTY OF IT ALL WEIGHS HEAVILY

My favorite virtual place is the I-Ching Online. Even though the horrible esoteric design of the site has none of the charm and ceremony of the book, you have the option of tossing the coins by hand, or virtually, which saves time and having to look for your change purse. I usually choose the virtual option because I have no time for ceremonies and no desire to scatter coins. I feel a little like a player addicted to Candy Crush, except I've never liked those sorts of games and I can't stand getting those online invitations. The I-Ching's answers are usually quite ambiguous and elusive because you can relate them at whim to whatever's worrying you. Yesterday I went online at four in the afternoon. I found a blank page that read: "Server access blocked due to excessive traffic."

"So right now there must be a throng of people anxious about their future," I said to myself. As the afternoon draws to a close, that throng – of which I am one – starts to experience a vertigo in which family, romantic, and work problems repeat in an eternal return. We consult the I-Ching so it will give us an answer, any answer, but above all:

"If you do what's right, everything will work out fine."

ADVANTAGES

The advantages of having a brother with a high degree of dependency is that you can't let yourself go. Unlike children with Down's syndrome, who have a certain autonomy, lower life expectancy and a disability that is visibly appropriate for advertising campaigns and jobs in companies that want to make a display of their solidarity, autistic people can have a perfectly normal appearance and live as many years as anyone else. Some of my favorite artists have ended up committing suicide or dying young. That doesn't enter into my plans: first of all, what would happen to my brother in the future if I weren't around? That question, in my attempt to compensate for not being a *neurosurgeon-genetic-engineer-discoverer-of-the-reasons-for-autism* and therefore *discoverer-also-of-his-cure*, in addition to having a vocation as precarious as artist usually is, has aggravated things. I try to brace my clearly artistic résumé with multiple certified foreign languages, a second undergraduate degree – in Literature, what can you do – and a master's. This feeling of added responsibility is something that also happens to those who've lost a brother or sister as children: somehow the awareness that you have an opportunity that someone close to you doesn't have, means you are haunted by a feeling of not being able to let down your parents, who already have enough to deal with.

All of that, plus the recession of 2008, ended up leading me from jobless desperation to teaching. Teaching secondary school is an activity that causes people to pity you; some hide it better than others. An activity that doesn't enter into the plans of the samurai existence demanded of the artists' collective, propelled across continents by grants, exchanges, artists' residencies, etc. And if they do teach, it's as a "guest artist" leading a workshop, usually funded by municipal cultural departments, because the administration assumes that there aren't artists among the teachers but rather that they swoop in from the supposedly glamorous art world in order to empower the lumpen with Marxism, postcolonial thought and queer theory. I envy that life. Yes; for the explorations, places and people that I miss out on. I also imagine a reality in which before each teacher enters the classroom at the start of the year, a bigwig sent from the Department of Culture would introduce him or her to their future students with reverence:

"Allow me to introduce X, whose teaching practice is situated between performance, conference, and activism. X has a long creative trajectory, having presented 875 variations on the same subject – Mathematics – in 75 different situations: first thing in the morning and at dusk, before students from urban centers, from small towns, and at risk of marginalization. Let's welcome X with a warm round of applause!"

Delusions aside, there is an important element necessary for any creative activity: a constraint. So many of us have to get up at seven. The best part is that there are a lot more people here and that staves off our spleen. Perhaps that's counter-productive if you aspire to have an international career, but if what you aspire to is focus and being able to work without creating dependencies (my highest aspiration right now), it's a great advantage. These are some of my current limits: I get up at 6:45 a.m., work until 2 p.m., and by 3 p.m. I'm home and can do whatever I want.

AFTER-DINNER CONVERSATION

"I would have children if, as I introduce them into the world, I could ask them if they want to be born," I say.

My mother's boyfriend, JR, a sixty-year-old philosophy professor, answers:

"I've already pondered this question. I came to the conclusion that, imagining infinite nothingness with suspended atoms, if any of those atoms had a moment of consciousness and could respond to the question of whether it wanted to exist, it would say yes, comparing the brevity of a human life with the long tedious eternity of a non-being. Existence, even if limited and filled with suffering, would seem like an adventure in the midst of that nothingness."

I'd always considered choosing to have children essentially an egotistical choice, based on earning emotional credits for old age and the biological necessity to continue our genes and relieve our loneliness. An option that is unnecessary for the planet, and inconsiderate toward the future being we bring into the world without asking for permission. In that sense, being born seems like signing a contract without having read its clauses. Growing up is gradually discovering them. Some of them are marvelous, others are terrible.

JR, a newcomer to the family, also exposes me to the other side of the question, what he calls "the egotism of not having children." In his own case, in which he didn't have them out of convenience, because he, in part, shares my opinion, and above all because of his ex-wife's wishes. A decision that JR now, sixty years old, regrets.

The possibility of having children without sufficient resources, not only economic but also in terms of family, sometimes seems irresponsible to me. But where is the line of what is considered sufficient? Is it that below a certain income per capita, and without a partner or available family, you shouldn't have kids? In other words, is the option to have children only for the fortunate and for normative families? And if not, how can parents be made aware of the dangers of transmitting behaviors that lead to poverty, illness, or unhappiness in an endless circle . . . ?

None of the arguments in favor or against convinces me entirely; I once again arrive at my usual state of permanent doubt and suspension of judgment. Every case is different. For the moment, I am too fond of my small apartment, my freedom (despite the doses of loneliness it brings) and my dance classes to consider the question very seriously. Conquering those basic things took fourteen years of my adult life.

SPOILED CHILDREN

Indulgent love on the part of a father or mother can also be a form of negligence; parents without limits and rules, who turn a blind eye to their child's defects, who idolize them so much that they are unaware of their real problems, are also guilty of a form of neglect.

R'S CLOSET

You often don't tidy up until you invite guests over to your house. And no one but me has gone into your walk-in closet in the last few years. Spring, summer, autumn, winter, year after year the clothing from your childhood and teenage years just kept getting hidden toward the back. Season after season you just superficially folded the visible part, with the clothes you wear every day, the essentials that occupy the small illuminated part of the room. Because, after all, you are the only one who goes in there. Until someone, me for example, tries to enter with a torch after seeing that you have holes in your socks, and searching for pajamas finds bras in the underwear drawer. The bras have a hook that pulls out some stockings with a run, curled up inside a jumper your gran knitted for you. The jumper has a button that you liked to touch, and it reminded you of the boy you used to play football with (wrinkled up, it's a nest for dust bunnies). And from inside the sleeve comes a balled-up black sock that was your father's – he was so obsessed with insisting you be punctual, and finished school – and further back, those pajamas, the Mickey Mouse ones they bought you when you all went to Disneyland together the summer right before the separation. All the way at the back, on the upper part of the last shelf, the bedspread with colorful edging that was always on your bed at your mother's house takes up a lot of space.

"Kid, organize your closet."

THE PRIZE

The gallery calls to tell me that I've been awarded a prize for my first solo exhibition, which I mounted the previous year. The ceremony is on Tuesday at the Barcelona Museum of Contemporary Art. I have a sore throat and I'm emotionally exhausted after a Christmas of arguments with R. An hour before the award ceremony I get out of bed, put on a white shirt buttoned all the way up and some black jeans. The shirt is semi-transparent and is patterned with tiny black lightning bolts. I keep losing weight. I take the metro there. When I arrive, I find the press there ready for a photocall. A television host is wearing a dress that looks like it's made of aluminum foil. I stand in a corner like the catering staff. The hall is filled with infinite white tables, elegantly set for the dinner with no one seated at them. They remind me of the story of Goldilocks – I'm an imposter, they're going to kick me out of the house. I look over at the photographers on a dais with a black backdrop covered in logos. They wait impatiently; no one has stepped up yet. I don't know any of the few attendees who've arrived. A guy as solitary as me stands waiting in one corner. We received the same grant for young emerging artists a couple of years ago. When he had won every grant available in this city he went to a country in northern Europe. We greet each other and he says, "Do you mind sticking with me? I'm feeling lost."

We go outside to smoke. He smokes, I just pretend to (I don't know why I can't refuse a cigarette). He was awarded this prize the previous year, this year he's a member of the jury. They pay for his flight and a hotel room as big as an apartment – he shows me photos on his mobile. He voted for me.

"Congratulations on the show. Why don't you apply for the same grant and come up north?"

He looks naturally elegant, not in a phony way, in his white shirt and jacket bought for the occasion. He has a small, already greenish, tattoo over his ear. A revolutionary star. I ask him how he ended up in Barcelona, moving from his home country.

"I'd heard good things about it. I lived in a squat for a few months, and I ended up sleeping on the street. Until P gave me the chance to show my work."

His art is a commentary on capitalist society, from the outside. It deals with the recession in Spain, politicians' false promises, the paradoxes and perversions of the neoliberal system.

"That led to MA asking for all the work I had. Soon he had sold it all at various international fairs."

That night I dream that we do it, him entering me from behind, standing on the white steps of the museum.

OBJECTS

I find the clothing you gave me everywhere, R. It envelops my body, contains my feet and when I go to pay, it's the leather wallet. In winter, shoes; in summer, trousers; when I pull out the coat I rarely wear, a shirt appears hung underneath it. Perhaps you don't even remember all these things that embrace me, that were "ours." When you were out of work, I worried about you impulsively buying things you thought would please me. Despite that, I accepted those gifts with the same equivocal feeling I had when my father, on the dole, would take us to a restaurant. That sense of excitement mixed with uncertainty and guilt. How could I accept them? Why did you give me all those gifts? Now I regret not having been the one to give them to you: clothes, shoes, perfume. Everything that could prolong my presence in you.

Because objects last longer than feelings.

BERGLUST[13]

Ice shrinks the veins and capillaries that bring blood to an injured area. As a consequence, the hematic flow – the blood – lessens. To put it another way, the ice calms the pain of knocks. Perhaps that's where tormented souls' preference for icy places comes from, the peacefulness of the snow falling. The indifference of the mountains. The beginning and end of Frankenstein, at the North Pole. Life in the mountains is trapped by something more serene and stable, purer and more elevated than life by the sea could ever be. In *The Philosophy of Landscape*, Georg Simmel states that the sea acts out of *empathy* toward life, and the Alps do so out of *abstraction*. This effect increases progressively as the rocky landscape gives way to the snowy.

Mini-breaks to the snow, like those to the beach, usually juxtapose the magnificence of the landscape against human banality. There is a common element in the way we inhabit these places: a stretch of nature is domesticated so we can

[13] Derived from the German expression "Wanderlust"; here it's "Berglust," the lust for mountains.

imagine that we are exploring it without much risk – the less apparent danger, the more mass tourism. You queue up for the ski lift, or to get a table at the bar; there are families and people dressed in bright colors. Music echoes through the snow. Silence must be avoided. The music is the same at ski resorts as in beach bars. You can go freestyle off-piste or swim past the buoy. Sometimes there are avalanches. Or a giant wave. The music tries to get us to forget about that. Obscuring our ephemerality in the face of the eternity of the seas and mountains, chopping up time into tiny pieces, as brief as a rhythm, a rhythm that gives time another meaning, one that is much more livable and fun.

Ice calms the pain of knocks, but if you ice a wound too long, the result can be detrimental. According to the *British Journal of Sports Medicine*, ice "does anaesthetise the area so that the patient does not feel pain, but nor does he feel that he is freezing the affected area of skin." The insensitivity can damage the healthy skin around the wound. I need to finish this project soon.

BLACK MIRROR

R apologizes, appeals, advances, retreats, pleads. He is the protagonist of a big performance, acted out in solitude behind the screen. No one, not even him, knows what's hidden behind the curtains of that show. His suffering, amplified on the social networks, attains catharsis 2.0 with a large number of likes.

ALPS

There was an airplane accident today in the Alps. A hundred and fifty people died. The plane crashed in the mountains. Peaks emerging in the passengers' windows. No natural or human landscape is invulnerable to terror anymore.

FEBRUARY, AGAIN

New visit to TD. He's changed offices to a main floor apartment uptown. Visiting that part of the city reminds me once again that this service, just like the stores on the corner, is a luxury. The room where we talk now has more light. The African masks have traveled from his other office. The shelves bulging with books and the divan have also come with him; my suspicion that it could be a shared office goes up in smoke. All the staging elements have been carefully selected. The red curtains are new, giving the large room a theatrical air. Beside the armchair where TD sits, right behind the psychoanalyst's face, hangs a particularly long mask with pointed features, and deep hollows for eyes. Magical elements far from the aseptic settings and positivism of Western medicine convert the visit into a ritual act. I ask him about the masks:

Etymologically, *person* comes from the Latin *persona*, mask, and is linked to "per-sona," that which sounds, relating to an actor's voice projection in a stage play. It references the particular role we occupy in life, unlike "human being," which alludes to what we all have in common.

TD is a mediator between a person and what is behind the mask. That hidden part is reached through that which sounds, the word.

"Okay . . . I'm listening."

". . . [I tell him about my breakup with R.]"

"R is merely a representative."

". . . ?"

"Those pros and cons were a reprise."

". . . ?"

"Perhaps by identifying the limits that are fundamental to you: Yes/no, white/black. And not only in relationships, also in other realms."

". . . ?"

"Realizing how much and how it affects us. Then knowing what place one occupies."

". . . ?"

"It seems to me that not adapting is being able to express what one feels."

". . . ?"

"It's clear that taking refuge is valid, but, with all due respect, it wasn't enough."

"The two relationships are very relevant. They both involved a certain refuge-taking. Refuge from what?"

"Refuge from my family."

"That is a very strong emotion. It has been controlled for a long time. But while dikes can remain in tension for a long time, one can liberate oneself, allow for flow . . . What would happen if I were to tell you that your paternal family has to do with a representation that perhaps has to do with one of a maternal family and that they converge in you? In the maternal one, you cannot be vulnerable, and therefore protected, in the other, there is no place for the possibility of self-expression."

Two tears stain my blue dress.

A TRIP TO ANTARCTICA

Icebergs' colors tell us something about their ice's origin and longevity. Gray icebergs could denote they were formed in a volcanic region, while intensely blue ones show that the ice is very old, since the immense pressure pushes the air out from inside (making the ice filter out all the colors except blue). I have seen several blue icebergs, and one in particular caught my eye because it was shaped like a dragon and was struggling against the waves during a rough storm that was trying to devour it. But one day I had the privilege of seeing something truly exceptional. Sailing around Antarctica, it is rare for scientists to come across a green iceberg. Their emerald color almost turns them into precious stones, with tones that acquire, depending on the slant of the light and its penetration, a wide spectrum of greens. [. . .] What in the past had been a green giant (at least at its base), was being tossed around, licked by waves in a slow but sure extinction. It was an old iceberg, about to be definitively consumed by the implacable persistence of the sea, which finishes off each and every iceberg by gradual erosion. Those who have had the opportunity to study these icebergs have found iron, copper, and other metallic elements within them. Young icebergs can trawl along the sea floor picking up particles that can remain inside them. It is not clear how this process occurs. Little by little, they erode and, like all icebergs, end up turning over. Then they reveal their bellies, which hold these metals. But that is not all that is found inside them, since a series of microscopic organisms seem to also give them part of their color; diatoms and benthic foraminifera, small fibers . . .

Another possibility is the existence of a series of parallel layers of green feldspar. Strong deep water currents and sediment resuspension – in other words, the fact that mud clouds the water at different moments – may have facilitated the incorporation of those elements, which would also explain why the layers are not uniform or homogenous. The icebergs' trawling and subsequent freezing due to temperature and pressure changes favor this incrustation.[14]

[14] Sergio Rossi, *Un viaje a la Antártida*, pp. 57–60.

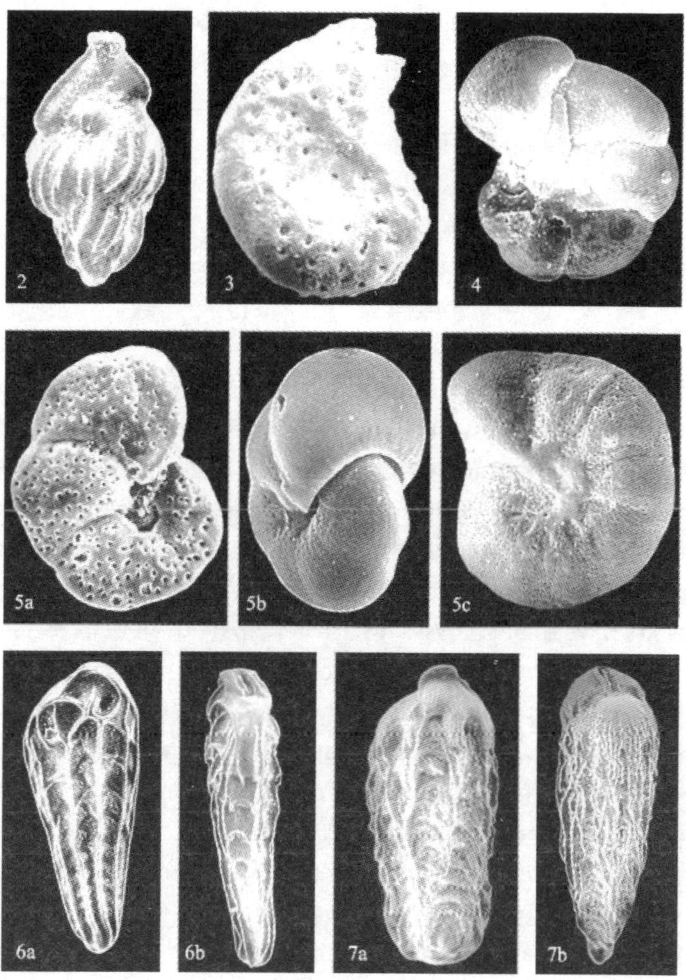

Benthic foraminifera from south central Chile (36°S–44°S). Source: the scientific journal *SciELO* http://www.scielo.cl/scielo.php?script=sci_arttext&pid=So717-65382005000200013.

Within the seemingly arid and barren environment of an iceberg, live beings with voluptuous, nourishing forms.

THE ILLOGIC OF ARCO

I show up at the art fair on Saturday morning. Paradoxically, being an art professional means I have to miss the days of the fair dedicated to art professionals. Like any other artist in this country who's beyond the post-adolescent phase and hasn't escaped a rent bill either via a family-owned apartment, squatting or Airbnb, I work during the week. These days artists have to be their own patrons. Apart from bankrolling my art, that slight petit-bourgeois delay will allow me to see the fauna who, like me, attend on a Saturday as part of the general public. When I arrive, my gallerist comes to greet me. We shake hands professionally and he hands me my accreditation. He reminds me that artists' presence at the stand is not particularly useful, ARCO is primarily a commercial event. But I'm not there to present my work, I want to see new things. We cover almost a kilometer on a moving walkway to reach Pavilion 9, where the gallery stand is located. He pulls out a Ducado; the tobacco choice of a generation that's giving way to the next. Once we're at the stand I'm received by his daughters, who give me water and practical tips to survive the crowds.

My work is located in front of a sketch of the project that Cabello/Carceller will do in Venice, and a painting by Lola Lasurt looking sidelong at a Julião Sarmento. The ultramaterial presence of another painting beside my piece provokes a certain repulsion in me – I can't help it: the material figuration is redundant. I note the viscous vibrations of the painting expanding out toward my fragile drawing. Like the franchise artists that are usually at ARCO – for example Julian Opie; I think I saw the same piece of his, in the same spot, ten years earlier – the fair is now well stocked with the franchises seen in most towns, including a Zara Men VIP Space converted into the Garden of Eden. The message is clear: you can only get to Eden if you pay more. Certain Catholic recollections appear in my little head, which was educated in secular schools. As I get older, I see that precisely because of that I am supremely naïve. That's real cynicism, not like Santiago Sierra's installations. Speaking of cynicism, I stop at ADN and ask for more details on a piece by Adrian Melis: a video in which a paper shredder does its job on reams of paperwork. The systematic destruction has a sadistic charm. Sadism can be erotic, the pages are precisely and intermittently sliced into strips. The gallerist tells me that the documents are résumés. The young woman destroying them was selected for the job through a listing posted by the artist himself: her job is to destroy the résumés presented by the other candidates. Like much of this kind of art that underscores power relationships in our society, what intrigues me most is the position of the subject – the young woman – in the action. She is a Bartleby-subject, someone who "would prefer not to" as he read the letters returned by the post office, letters which will never reach their intended recipients, likewise her résumés will receive no response.

There are several artists currently exposing the dynamics of capitalist work. Is exposing them while taking part in them cynical or does it somehow lead to greater awareness? Is there any critical form that has not been absorbed by the system? This question raises a series of reflections in my mind, making me walk distractedly, sidestepping the Madrid bourgeoisie and families who've come to see the glass half empty/half full (depending on how you look at it) by Wilfredo Prieto, all happy to see a work that is so easily reproducible at home. Without a predetermined itinerary, I walk in circles constantly stumbling on the same works and ignoring others that surely deserve more attention. Like in life itself, we always seem to be tripping over the same damn stone. This time I stumble upon Jonathan Millán at Estrany-de la Mota; his installation speaks to me snidely about the difficulty of autobiographical expression in the artistic environment. The title: *Awkward Family Moment*. A striking occasion pulled straight from the creator's life.

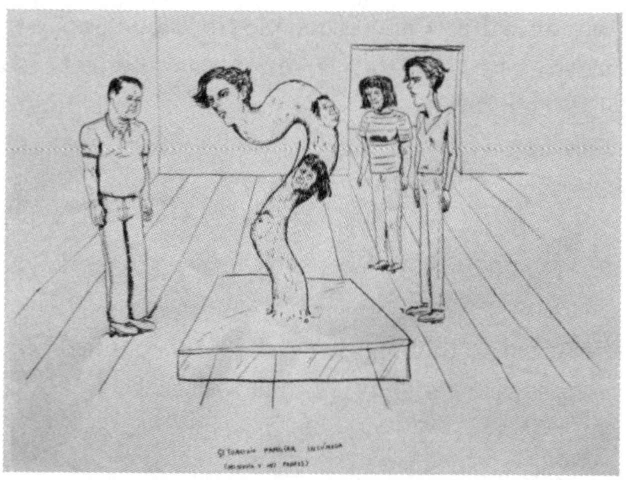

Awkward Family Moment, Jonathan Millán.

At Pavilion 7, Helga de Alvear presents us with the megalomaniacal paintings of Katharina Grosse. That artist, who was a teacher of mine during an exchange fellowship in Berlin in 2005, has evolved from a certain pictorial formalism to this current neo-sublime extravaganza. In the center of the space is a tree fallen onto pieces of polystyrene spray-painted in neon colors. Her personality and work is magnetic, exclusively "made in Germany" in both the aesthetic and the economic tradition. While with the former I'm clearly referring to the Romantic tradition, with the latter I mean the fact that she studied Fine Arts twice and then was hired by the university to teach without having a doctorate. (In Germany one's artistic trajectory is valued more than one's degrees.) A solid foundation for working, plus the Teutonic country's creative infrastructure; that's what I'm referring to when I say that the German cultural and economic tradition supports her. Her artistic résumés rarely mention that she teaches and is still studying. I wonder what prejudices are behind that omission, or whether including it would somehow cloud her hagiography.

MARCH 21, 2015

A German friend told me that Alicia Kopf sounded like the name of a Jewish émigré. I was fine with that.

MARCH 24, 2015

Today I had a dream in which R confessed to me that he'd worked as a gigolo. Once, he told me, a man paid to watch me masturbate. In the next scene of the dream I was using his computer and found a folder of photographs of cut-up bodies with wounds. The images were details, there were no whole bodies or faces. Only pubic areas, buttocks, and thighs of indeterminate gender, of pubescent individuals with cuts and scars. I wondered why he collected those photographs and suspected a perverse use. Later, I found myself stroking his face gently and telling him:

"Don't worry, I love you just the same."

MARCH 24, 2015

I start taking dance classes; I see things clearly when I'm dancing.

THE CHOREOGRAPHER

In class I fall on the spins, I lose my balance. I can't find my axis.

J: You need to cherish yourself more. Let yourself shine, use your gifts, stand up for yourself, show yourself, you don't know it but you can do it another way, transform it, you have a language.

(I fall.)

J: Look straight ahead. Find a fixed point on the wall and keep your eyes there.

(I turn.)

J: OK, that's it.

"How can you regain your balance when you've lost it?"

J: You have to dig deep. You can only find your balance when you can show your vulnerability and face your demons. That's the only way. It entails an exercise in humility. You won't be able to be honest or humble until there are no longer any traces of pretense in you.

J adopts the lecturing – not at all humble – tone he likes to adopt in these circumstances. After class I tell him what happened to me.

J: The problem with that person is that he wants to receive. And he gives objects without truly giving. He is giving you external things, he is giving you gifts to ensure reciprocation and to compensate for what he can't offer. A relationship can have an energy that feeds back into itself, or it can be a short circuit. The spark it gives off produces a lot of light but then leaves you in the dark. And you need the other person more and more to recover that light. As that repeats, you are left in progressively deeper, larger darknesses. That is the mechanism of addiction . . . What's his sign?

"Aquarius, like my father."

J: (Shakes his head, rolls his eyes with a heavy sigh, and laughs.) An Aquarian has to work very hard on individual human relationships, they can be adored on a group level, but face-to-face they have a lot of problems connecting.'

I don't personally believe in astrology, although I sometimes like to read my horoscope when I'm bored. But I have to admit that R's personality fit that profile perfectly. I explain that R is very skilled at communicating, and can turn around situations of conflict with ease so he becomes the victim. That doesn't mean that he has access to what he's truly feeling. He works hard in the world of music management, but he hasn't devoted any energy to working on himself, to figuring himself out. I have the feeling he's avoiding something.

J: That's typical of an Aquarius. Aquarius is an air sign, even though it circulates in the water element. There's a lot of emotiveness but it's not directed, they have a terrific ability to communicate, but it's not based on anything, it's pure air. They are the Greenpeace of the zodiac, the ones who help the weak whenever they can, who can move masses, those who can sacrifice themselves for a group cause, but when they get home they're unable to say "I missed you all day" or "You know what? I'm scared." Or simply, there will be things in the relationship that aren't working, but they'll never address them head-on, it will be obliquely. You understand what I mean?

"I recognize some of it," I reply, "but only after very serious arguments. And his desire is inconsistent in the same way. It's especially problematic when things are flowing smoothly. It doesn't work unless there's drama, or we haven't seen each other in a while. Not ever as a predictable thing. And I'm not talking about boredom. I'm talking how after a few months of a relationship you can lay your head on the other person's shoulder."

J: Hunt him down, challenge him, dominate him.

"You've watched too many music videos."

ICE BLINK

Ice blink is a white light that appears near the horizon, especially on the underside of low clouds, resulting from the reflection of light off a field of ice immediately below them. This luminous effect was valued by both the Inuit and explorers searching for the Northwest Passage, to help them find their orientation and navigate safely.

As I wonder about the journey or the plot guiding this narration, I sense that there's something I must discover, and until I do I won't be able to finish. There has to be a conquest. At this point the territory is not yet visible to me. If it were, I wouldn't write. This isn't a banal voyage, and it's no safer than the ones undertaken by the explorers: I feel that my life is at stake. Writers' prefabricated plots and characters are odd to me, as unknowable as the past and future of people I pass on the street. They come and go, often without us understanding the meaning behind their arrivals or departures. They carry their plots inside them, and often do not include us in the figures they are creating. The actions of others, and sometimes our own, are a mystery to us. Third-person narrations are security fences. Omniscient narrators, pure arrogance. Perhaps I think that because I'm not an author, just an explorer of my limited textual possibilities. Narration as a place to fictionalize memory, which is constructed, partial, voluble, and will be reinvented in the text and therefore always destroyed again in the text. That ax we use to break the frozen sea that inhabits us.

Symzonia.

PARIS

MARCH 29, 2015

Presentation of my work for a conference on contemporary art at the Sorbonne Nouvelle. Expenses paid by the Institut Ramon Llull.

It seemed like it was going to rain the whole week but the sun comes out occasionally. H and Ma, a couple of friends who live in a garret at 33 Boulevard de Clichy, let me stay in a double room with views of the Sacré Cœur and Montmartre.

I bring some homework with me; I'm preparing the translation of my first book. Opening those files took me a couple of days and a rainy morning. Finally I revise the text and send it to the translator.

Right before I came I cleared the memory on my iPhone so I could take more photos. The program transferred the thousands of photos taken over a year onto my computer. That new folder contains the entire space of time that my relationship with R lasted. Like that effect they say happens at the moment of your death when your life flashes before you, nine months with R parade before my eyes in just a few minutes. In the photos where we're on holiday, he is always sleeping; in the hotel, on the beach, on the lounge chairs of the restaurant. The camera outlines details of his body: his hands, his knees, the corner of his mouth, the inner part of his arm, his closed eyes.

MARCH 29, 2015

Lately, during the boring parts of conferences and colloquiums, I think about sex. I wonder if the other attendees are doing the same. Now I write in my notebook as if the speaker had said something very interesting.

L'HOMME PARISIEN

Morning. Le Pain Quotidien. Everyone seems busy writing a novel here in Paris. In the café I'm at there are people working on their computers, like me, or reading. Part of me would like to be at home, to have a family life. The other wants adventure. I haven't yet found anyone who can accompany me in both things. It would be amazing to live here for a while. Improve my French. Not work much. Have fun. Watch life from a small round café table.

Afternoon. Le Progrès café, rue de Bretagne, the heart of the Marais.

A guy comes up to me. He seems very French; dirty blond hair and gray eyes. He asks me if he can sit at my table and we chat a little. He is nice, says that he's an actor. He's quite a bit younger than me. He's surprised when I tell him my age. Thirty must be some sort of a psychological barrier for him. But he isn't scared off. We talk about the theater. Night falls, the actor chivalrously walks me to the house of my friend JM, from my high school days, who has invited me over for dinner.

He insists we meet up some other day.

Why isn't attraction always mutual? It should be.

"*Merci, adieu.*"

APRIL 3, 2015

I make a plan with JM and his roommate, A, to have dinner out. It's late and all the restaurants are closing. I'm wearing my hair straight and shoulder-length – usually it's long and naturally wavy. I have the feeling that until I was thirty I never styled my hair, I was too busy with my schoolwork and projects. We finally find a restaurant on Rue de Bretagne, in front of Le Marché des Enfants Rouges, and near Le Progrès, where I was approached by the actor. We sit down at one of the small tables outside, warmed by an overhead heater. A goes out for a smoke and we see him outside talking to a thirty-something man with black hair. JM sits beside me, elegant as always. He has on a white shirt with a narrow black tie and leather fingerless gloves.

When A comes back to the table he tells me that the guy he was talking to had asked about me: whether I was with him or with JM, and what we were doing that night. He told him that he'd lived all over the world, before finally returning to his native Paris. The guy looks at us from his table, a few meters away.

Disconcerted, I don't react. The guy, who is there with another man, turns every once in a while in our direction; they've already finished their meal. Finally they leave. When the guy stands up, I find him attractive.

The night continues, we go to a few different places and then to Silencio, a club set up by David Lynch. The music is good and we dance a lot. I imagine what could have happened if I'd gotten up from the table to say hi.

APRIL 4, 2015

I wake up late. I go to the Palais de Tokyo. Visitors are greeted by a large-scale piece called "JUST SAY NO TO FAMILY VALUES." It is the title of a text by John Giorno adapted to a large format by Sowat. I meet up with JM again, today he shows me the Left Bank. It's raining. Since he has to leave for work later he leaves me on the Boulevard St. Germain and recommends a café: Le Hibou. It's a sophisticated place, like many of the ones my friend frequents; thanks to his wealthy family he's always been able to live the life of a postmodern dandy. I arrive, close my umbrella and dry off at one of the narrow tables warmed by heaters hanging from the awnings. It seems like sitting at outside tables is an important activity for Parisians, who are out in equal numbers rain or shine. A couple of French guys two rows away turn brazenly toward me. They say something to each other and one of them leaves. The one remaining is blond, his slightly long hair brushed back, with melancholic blue eyes and a thin moustache. He's wearing a suit jacket with small brown and green plaid with elbow pads; all that's missing is a flower in his buttonhole.

As time passes the axis of his torso rotates; instead of looking at the street he has now turned his profile in my direction. Men have a very sensitive radar for women's energy. The law of attraction depends exclusively on that, on the energy that is given off at certain moments. Expectation mixed with confidence is one of the energies that attracts them most, and these days in Paris have me glowing. It doesn't happen to me often, that feeling that some call self-confidence even though it's not exactly the same thing. He picks up a book and seems to be very focused on taking notes, but still keeps his head lifted in my direction. A woman arrives and sits down next to him. She's wearing a lot of makeup, and clothing and accessories with expensive brand logos, all so ostentatious that they could be fakes. Her long black hair reaches her waist and is slightly scorched from so much straightening. A few seconds later she takes his head in her hands and kisses him passionately. He seems to accept it willingly, albeit passively. Shortly after, she rummages through her bag, looking for something and she gets up on her way to the bathroom. He turns toward me again with the book in his hand; he hasn't put it down at any point. He looks at me, and he smiles at me. I smile back, open my umbrella, and leave.

I imagine a secret local community of bookish gigolos living off of the romantic fantasies of wealthy young women.

WHATSAPP

APRIL 5, 2015

[R:] You look very pretty in your whatsapp photo.

Thanks. C'est Paris.

(End of the conversation.)

APRIL 14, 2015

[R:] Today would be our one-year anniversary. I'll wait for you at the restaurant where we first had dinner together. If you don't come I won't bother you again.

I can't. Maybe another day.

(End of the conversation.)

APRIL 19, 2015

I return to the routine of teaching. On Friday I'm called into the principals' office in the middle of a class. The two principals of that elite school tell me that they are happy with me but that they need more English teachers. They indicate to me with their attitude that there is no possibility of negotiation or further explanation. I try to ask for reasons but they repeat what they've already said. That I will finish out the year and they will terminate my contract. That I shouldn't worry, they will give me very good references.

"Okay."

I go back to class. The kids are working serenely. Last hired, first fired; the cheapest one to let go of, even when there's a steady contract; it's very easy these days to get rid of an employee. Luckily I don't have a mortgage and haven't even really considered having children . . . maybe they chose me just for that reason . . . The woman who does the remedial classes, and who's involved with the owner of the school wanted my language class . . . If they give that one to her and the other to my colleague in the department, they'll save one salary . . . Any mistake I could have made, any setback . . . They can always find some reason. Someone take me away from here, far away.

APRIL 20, 2015

> [Me, in a WhatsApp to R:] OK. Let's get together. Take me to the sea.

APRIL 23, 2015

R picks me up in his mother's sports car. He is wearing a shirt with small white flowers on a navy blue background that he bought last summer when we were on holiday, and jeans, and yellow sneakers that match the car. His look, this time, is somewhere between comic and working-class.

"I was dying to see you," he says. His enthusiasm sometimes borders on the manic.

During lunch, in an expensive restaurant at some port in the Maresme, he reasserts himself:

"I'm sure: I want to be with you."

He gets up from the other side of the table and kisses me passionately. His lips are fleshy and fickle, and with the enthusiasm of the moment they heat up very quickly, becoming warm and welcoming. But they can cool off just as quickly. That's the case with every part of his body and his soul. We end up in bed together.

APRIL 24, 2015

Today he isn't so sure.

JUNE 1, 2015

Swamped with work; classes, an exhibition and a new edition to revise, translate, and send to press. I swallow my pride and show up punctually to work every day, as if nothing has happened. Someone else might have raised Cain over being let go without good reason, but I can't take the risk of losing my right to unemployment because of a disciplinary offense (which they could claim if they didn't want to arrange for my papers). On the other hand my students aren't to blame, so I try not to let them notice. The woman who does the remedial classes asks me for my syllabus for next year; she will be teaching my subject. Rumors spread through the school and the kids ask me if it's true that the owner and their future teacher are having a thing.

In an attempt to cheer myself up after recent events, I ask my mother if she could organize a lunch with friends at the house. She says no without any logical reason. She has to clean before the renters arrive. I tell her that we can eat in the garden, and that she has a whole month before they get there. The answer is "no." The wall of authoritarianism, the steamroller. Rain of ash. I'm thrown back into my adolescence. The situation relived now, and already lived thousands of times, takes me back to the deepest pit of my high school years, pummeled with punishments for my rebelliousness. Because I always "asked for too much," and because "it's not possible." I will never know if I got through those years despite her or thanks to her. I call R to ask for consolation, consolation which he gives me coldly. The next day he sends me some messages that suggest something isn't going right. I call him in the middle of important tasks, thinking that it's urgent. R tells me over the phone that he's scared. That he doesn't feel able to give me what I need. That it's best if we leave it be. I ask him coolly if he's aware that this sudden change of opinion dynamites a year-long relationship. He says yes. I say goodbye calmly, the way I do when I'm overwhelmed by situations and I save them to deal with later. I finish work, go out and get my scooter. I explode inside the helmet, the crying helmet.

I placed my foot on very thin ice. First I slipped. Now I'm sinking.

JUNE 3, 2015

Moments of sun alternate with gusts of pain and longing that cut through my chest with the whimper of a dog that's been run over.

RAGE AND THAW
PYRENEES MINI-BREAK

Friday night. I have a completely free weekend ahead of me, perfect for frittering away in see-sawing emotions – rage-longing-rage-longing – and wasting time on social media, and finally going to see my family mostly just to remember I have one. I get an email from G, who I haven't seen much for a long while, perhaps since the last time I was single, four years ago. I call her and she says that she's going up to the Pyrenees that very evening. That she'll spend the night there with a friend and his dog.

"Is it a date?" I ask her.

"No."

G's friends are very different to the ones in my circles, normally tied to the cultural sector.

"Pack a bag quickly, we'll come pick you up."

I don't have any equipment, and am quite the city mouse, but I improvise a rucksack best I can. She brings me a sleeping bag and mat. G is impulsive, almost to the point of recklessness. She went by herself to the Himalayas. In many regards I would say that she is the person I know who is most my opposite. I say that because of her explosive power – as opposed to my British unflappability – combined with a certain, very punctual malice. G, however, is always willing to help others in difficult moments. I, on the other hand, am usually focused on my projects, and that leads people not to think of me as someone they can count on. In a family where the mother always works, the father's not around, and there's an autistic brother, it's best to entertain yourself. G grew up with four siblings, and is used to working in a team. She is one of those people who show up for moving day and at hospitals, and usually have their doors open. That is highly prized in this era of people alone in front of their computers.

It doesn't strike me as terrifically prudent, but that's how G's plans are, and I want to see snow and mountains. Snow is always snow, and it's a way to maintain a link to *Arcticantarctic*, that place I'm trying to circumscribe with text and whose center I hope to someday conquer. On the way there, we are stuffed into a little car that smells of dog, along with the dog who's whimpering the whole time. The friend, who is also named R – I'll hear his name throughout the entire trip, as if he weren't only with me in my thoughts but also present in the words spoken around me – says that he works hand-polishing metals for prestigious jewelry makers. Now that everything is done by machine or in China, it hadn't occurred to me that such a job existed and was done in artisans' workshops in our country. The idea of polishing jewels is interesting, I think.

"What do you do with the remaining scrap material?"

"We have to give it back. Polishing is a type of erosion. They keep strict control over the weight of the precious materials, milligram by milligram."

I wonder if after all these years of study, work, and more or less failed relationships, I've been polishing myself or eroding myself. Is what's left a gem, or a rock?

I'm at my lowest weight. I'm back in a state of economic instability and I'm single. Right now, having a family seems remote. I may be wasting the decent salary I've had recently on a psychoanalyst, which has allowed me to finally rent an apartment in my own name and have four nice dresses. The psychoanalyst supplants the big question, the solution, to use his vocabulary, metonymically. I've reached the phase where I've structured my identity around "lack," but how can I change that? That question finds a perpetual answer in continuing therapy, in digging deeper. The only thing that gives me strength is writing: constructing meaning. Is it possible I get myself into all these problems just so I can later write about them? Did I believe in a dubious relationship to see where it would lead me, as a narrative? Perhaps my writing was calling me back, and I unconsciously detonated everything when I reached my limit? Writing is the poison and the antidote. Or as Lispector says, writing is a curse, but a curse that saves us.

At midnight we arrive at Bellver de Cerdanya and spend the first night at G's family's flat. The next day we have a bumpy ten kilometers to the Perafita Refuge, 2,500 meters above sea level. There we find ourselves at the finish line of a fifty-kilometer race through the mountains. We watch as the exhausted athletes arrive after ten hours on their feet. Our plan is a stroll. In mid-June, the day is overcast and showery, and amid the rocky masses and fir trees you can see the melting snow in its full spectrum of states: calm, stagnant, violent, transparent, clouded. Streams, waterfalls, small marshes camouflaged in the fluorescent green grass. A mountaineer tells us that we can drink the water but never when it's stagnant. I take note of his words, in many senses. Fuchsia flowers among the grass. We hear the bubbling of a nearby cascade. I wanted to cry anyway. I am a zombie Werther, wandering amid the firs after having fallen in love and shooting himself four times.

After an hour of ascent, we finally find the ultimate vestiges of the last snowfall of the season on the peak. That's where the descent begins, now amid rocks and sand again. On the way down one of my knees starts to hurt. We only remember our dependence on the body when it's not working. Luckily it's nothing serious and we get past the most irregular stretches. At a certain height firs, grass and brooks reappear on every side. Wet feet. It starts to drizzle and it's cold.

We occasionally pass some of the participants in the race, headed in the opposite direction. They have been walking for about eight hours. They stop for a moment to chat with us and we offer them dried fruit. There is a special solidarity in the mountains. Because we are all more aware of our fragility. Some of those passing in the opposite direction look like professional athletes. I exchange a glance with one of them who looks about my age; he has a black, quick gaze, beneath wavy damp brown hair stuck to his forehead. After a little while I turn and I see that he's turned too. Later we come across some other participants between fifty and sixty years old. Soon we can make out the roof of the refuge at the base of the valley, among the fir trees. It is one of the race's control points. There is a small group of people and a thin stream of smoke emerges from the small chimney. Before we reach the shelter we go through a terrain where the grass hides swampy patches. That rules out even the slightest possibility of keeping our feet dry. Lake, brooks, melted snow. Drizzle. Our dog leaps blissfully, takes the lead and lopes back to us, happy to be nowhere near asphalt.

MOUNTAIN REFUGE

We reach the refuge at four in the afternoon. We have five hours of daylight ahead of us, with absolutely nothing to do, unless we want to take a hike in the rain. The small hut is a cement square with metal bunk beds, an iron table in the middle, and a timid fireplace that struggles to stay lit with all the damp. The mystery of why the floor is soaking wet, despite the fire, is resolved with the discovery of a slow leak, with water snaking down right through the chimney. We will spend the night there, since we can't go any further. As we stretch out on the metal beds, it becomes clear that there is no position that doesn't lead to shoulder or hip pain, even with the mats.

There are fewer and fewer walkers from the race, until the sweeper car comes by and closes the control point. A foreign hiker couple arrives. As usual, G asks them a lot of questions, and they respond as best they can in basic, but well-intentioned English. They are Czech and are crossing the Pyrenees. They started at Cap de Creus and have been walking for a few weeks. He has a beard and long hair, she wears a handkerchief on her head. When she takes it off we realize they look alike: both of them have long blond hair, are of medium height, very thin and with very white skin. They must be in their thirties. They joke about how long it's been since their last showers. They work three months out of the year harvesting fruit in Italy and spend the rest of their time traveling. They have worn clothes and old backpacks. They barely have any food, and are happy to accept what we offer them. When we give them a handful of extra energy bars, she says:

"It's like Christmas."

And she smiles sincerely.

Shortly after we've tucked ourselves in we start to hear a stream of water falling directly from the center of the shelter's ceiling and splashing against the iron table. The fire went out some time ago and with it the hope that our sneakers will dry by the next day. The small refuge where it rains on the inside makes me think of the cover of my first book, where drops of water form a small house. I started it when I finished school, when the recession of 2008 was beginning. It talked about getting "no" as an answer when you want to enter the adult world of work and love. The project was well-received because of its fresh treatment of the subject of young people scraping out a living during the recession. "Fresh" enough to reach a wide audience despite the fact that I wrote it in a state of desperation. Controlled desperation, of course. Because in order to be able to express your feelings you have to be willing to destroy them by subjecting them to the laws of form. And when I think about it, that was how I survived that period; because I worked on those obsessions until they were no longer mine, until they were nothing more than pure form that creates meaning and that ultimately, if you are both skilled enough and honest enough, forges a connection with others. The world was slamming doors in my face and I thought: I will call it out and I will laugh. I won't cry and I won't complain. I will keep drawing and writing. After all, I have no mortgage and I more or less have a roof over my head. But there were people who weren't able to do that. Some threw themselves onto the tracks. There were those who said my project was ironic. But there is nothing more dangerous than irony in a state of emergency. Irony implies accepting the negativity of the situation itself, it implies incorporating the "lack." It's sketching a half-smile and staying out in the downpour. That is why institutions can't accept irony in its most negative form, cynicism; nothing can be built under its banner. There can be no cynicism in a hero, a leader, or a family. As soon as there is, everything rots. I copied the slightly naïf tone of that book's texts and drawings from an advertising agency selling apartments from the bank. The apartments many people were evicted from, the apartments many people cannot enter. That is real cynicism.

I hear the water falling in the middle of the little refuge. The Czech couple sleeps huddled together on an iron bed. Their sleep is sweet.

We wake up with the sun, the couple has already left to continue their journey through the Pyrenees. The valley awakens beneath a transparent sky. The dawn's slanted light lengthens the shadows of the rocks with an angle I've never seen before.

PILLS

I don't know if I should wait for the wound to scar up or simply take a mental holiday. I think about anti-depressants. It would be good to be happier.

But, excluding serious pathologies, I have the feeling that a lot of people take pills to tolerate situations that are often largely not their responsibility, or at least not theirs alone but rather collective, social. Like being trapped in an alienating job with no way out . . . or on the dole with no way out . . . or in a family with no way out . . . or in a present with no future . . . or a victim of betrayal . . . or being made redundant . . . Those pills that numb the pain might also be staving off the collapse of the system. They keep people from going out onto the street and asking for help and placing blame, keep them from fighting, the pills avoid conflict, but maybe also avoid solutions. Because as soon as we ask others to smile, be happy, close that chapter, take pills, frigging keep calm and carry on, we are complicit in the situation. I won't take them.

GEYSER

I ask my mom if she can drive me to IKEA one day. She says that she'll try to figure out a time. A week later she hasn't said anything and I have no more days off before my trip. Finally I call her and she says that, yes, in the end she can come, but she doesn't know what time and she doesn't know how to get there, and she's not sure about this or that. I say thanks, OK, I'll figure out the route, but is it really necessary to keep me waiting so many days for something so simple. It's been a year and a half since I moved to this apartment and no one in my family has yet asked me if I need anything. When she recently fixed up the country house, I spent a month painting walls. I gave her some furniture from the apartment I was leaving, I bought her curtains and some kitchen stuff for Christmas. I tell her I don't understand that disparity, why she finds so many obstacles to helping me with something so simple. She says yes, she's on her way and I shouldn't complain. But the wait has set me off and I'm angry. I put off asking for help too long, and now I'm irritable. I ask her why I always have to beg for things that so many families offer easily. She repeats that she's on her way, that I shouldn't complain, that she had trouble arranging things at work to get away. I answer that it's her own problem she prioritizes her work the way she always has, that it's late July and most teachers aren't anywhere near school. She gets mad and says that I shouldn't criticize her work, that I don't know what her obligations are, that she can't just not show up, that she's the director. I get tired of her not understanding the basis of my argument: it's not about her coming now but that it hasn't occurred to her that I might need help in the year and a half since I moved, and now she's doing it with gritted teeth because I insisted. By this point I'm crying and I throw the telephone on the couch. She writes me a message:

"I'm really sorry, sweetie! I told you on Monday I'm all yours. And maybe we haven't done things the way we should have . . . In fact, today I'm very tired . . ."

"I'm sorry I got mad but I feel like I have to beg for things that are easy in other families."

"No, babe, we love you very much in this family." I'm intrigued by her use of the plural, the family is small and I'm not in touch with most of its members. I guess my brother loves me but I don't have much empirical proof.

"That doesn't count if it's just words."

"No, sweetie, we can't compare ourselves to others, everyone has their own issues, and if you think about it when you've cooled off you'll see we aren't that bad. I'm so sorry you feel like this. I think maybe you are too alone."

"I'm not comparing, I'm just saying what I see."

"But you are just looking on the surface."

"Helping someone isn't superficial at all. Loving from a distance and thinking that everybody else has to figure it all out on their own is the same as not loving them."

"Sweetie! That's not true. You can come home whenever you want."

"I don't want to come home because it's not my home. My room is a dark hole, it's the junk room. A room where you came in and out and changed the decoration whenever you felt like it. That's why I left at seventeen."

"Honey, you know that isn't true. I don't know what you're after with these false accusations that don't get us anywhere. Oh, and I am who I am, and look, if I don't have enough money to make you feel a little satisfied with life, I don't know what to say. You should know that I've been working since I was eight, when I worked at home, to have what I have. I'm sorry but you're going too far."

"I'm not talking about money. I'm not talking about how you are either. What I'm saying is that you haven't offered me what you asked for in your house."

"Oh, and about M. He's disabled, in case you've forgotten, and I've suffered with that for the last forty years and I don't complain. And you were labeled highly gifted at the age of six." Stupefaction. That's new to me. "And you think that's NOT enough in this life? Is that nothing? And parents who love you but aren't perfect." She must not remember that my father has barely spoken to me in the last ten years. "But you are perfect, right? Have you thought about that? Some of us have got through life with much less and look at us, we're fine . . . because you have to look forward and be satisfied with what you have, otherwise it's very hard to be a little happy. I only had my father and I haven't spent my whole life complaining about that."

"So I see I have to pay for my brother and for your childhood. Thanks for everything you didn't give me to compensate for everything I got without even knowing."

"Come on, you aren't paying for anything, you're just complaining. Don't say such things. You have no idea what paying even is. And believe me, people have enough work with just staying afloat and they don't think about all that stuff."

"Look, Mom, I don't think I got most of the things other kids get: being picked up from school, not having to wander alone through the city at the age of eight to go to afterschool activities. Having to go through my parents' separation alone and without psychological support from my family or school, cooking since I was twelve for my nineteen-year-old brother, etc."

"And you are still talking nonsense. Have you stopped to look at people on the street, not the privileged, but the ones who struggle over things that you can't even imagine?! Of course it's easier to look in the mirror and compare yourself to people who are better off and start in with 'oh, poor me!' No, my dear, I realize you are going through a rough time, but believe me: you are wrong. Otherwise, I'll have to think I raised a girl who is incapable of fighting and keeping her nose to the grindstone when things aren't going well."

"I am fighting, but it's you who doesn't want to look in the mirror. Listen to what I'm telling you, instead of sweeping the crap under the rug. Then I'll be better."

"Look, we all have bad days. If it makes you feel better to think that I'm a monster, and so is everyone around me, go right ahead. But believe me, when everyone is wrong except you, that's a sign of a problem! That's right! We're all monsters and you're an angel, sure!"

"I didn't say that, you prefer your misinterpretation over actually listening to me. All I'm saying is that you neglected me because of some supposed abilities of mine that somehow exempted you from responsibility. And I have to beg for normal things. Like you driving me to IKEA one day during the summer break."

I didn't mean for it to go that far. I want to go to my studio.

"No, that's not it!! We figure that you are old enough and if you don't ask for help it's because you can do it on your own." That plural is making me more and more uneasy, who is she referring to this time? Her boyfriend has an opinion about my possible needs? Why is it that our parents' new partners always think we're old enough to figure things out on our own? Haven't I been doing that for years now? "Oh, and don't start with this bull, I didn't come to you talking about monsters and bad families. You are the one who comes up with these stories you know aren't true. If you want to keep blaming everyone else for what's happened to you, go right ahead . . . but it's hard to be happy like that . . . You know that I'll be there on Monday, that at the end of the day I'm your mother and I love you more than anyone. And if you need money, we'll dig some up, don't worry."

I wonder what brought on that burst of generosity.

I repeat: "I am not asking for money. And asking for a ride to IKEA shouldn't have to mean begging on my hands and knees."

"OK, fine, you know that sometimes money is the least of it."

"I'm talking about a car ride. I've rented a van several times, but I thought that since it's summer you could help me out."

"Enough! We've talked enough. M is about to arrive and I have to shower him, shave him, dress him . . . And believe me, no one does my work for me, and you don't hear me complaining."

The conversation ends with her sending me a few heart emoticons. It's her new way of shutting me up. I spend the rest of the evening disoriented. I couldn't care less about her revelation, which after all is pseudoscientific and from twenty-seven years ago. What frightens me are the twenty-seven years my mother kept quiet about it and what that silence means. The certainty that I've been paying for something that's not my fault overwhelms me. *Arri arri tatanet, que anirem a Sant Benet, comprarem un formatget i per a la nena no n'hi haurà.*[15] I'm tempted to call R. I miss him. It's really hot and I can't sleep. I fall asleep late. I'm awoken the next morning by my own crying.

On Monday my mother shows up at my place with the car. It's the first time she's come since I moved a year and a half

[15] Children's song: "Giddy up, little horsie, we're going to Sant Benet, where we'll buy a little cheese, though for the little girl there'll be none."

ago. We go to IKEA and she seems happy to help me. I ask her why she'd never told me that about school. She says that it wasn't anything definite, there were no documents and after she spoke with other teachers and specialists they advised her not to pay much attention to it. Later it was decided that I didn't have the highest points in every aspect, particularly in mental arithmetic. At the time that label was only given to those who had the highest points in every area. The public school didn't have the means to serve such a distinction, so my mother decided to let it go.

"The criteria for those things is very unclear, there are many types of intelligence."

"That's true. I think if I took the test now I wouldn't even be borderline," I say, taking into account the romantic errors I've made in the last few years, my tendency toward self-sabotage and my self-exile through irony.

DID YOU SLEEP WELL?

About five years ago my mother started to rent out the country house during the summers, and that was the beginning of our tradition of spending a week on the coast. With the separation, both my parents were strapped with their respective rent and mortgage payments, so there were no summers at the beach or trips during the long period between eight and twenty years old. After that we were on our own. This recently inaugurated week at the beach is an experience of living with my mother, my brother, and now, my mother's boyfriend. Apart from the pleasure of being near the sea, this holiday usually serves to remind me how much attention M still needs at forty: waking him up, dressing him, giving him breakfast. Once he's eaten, he has to be told to either sit on the sofa or wait in some particular place because otherwise he just stands there waiting, not knowing what to do. If he needs a shower you have to undress him and help him. He can be left alone during these tasks but then you run the risk that he gets stuck in some sort of stand-by mode, suspended in the midst of the action. If he is showering he stays under the stream of water indefinitely, with the risk that the water could get cold and so would he. If he is dressing, he could get stuck with his T-shirt on his hands looking through the hole where his head should go, in position to put it on, but with no guarantee as to when he will actually do so; he might take five minutes, an hour, or three. So, in the normal day-to-day, and because of the schedules of other people who work and can't have the bathroom tied up for two hours, they end up doing or helping him do most things. Other people, primarily my mother, are his "prosthesis" for taking those little everyday decisions that most of us take without realizing. That is his survival strategy; we are a sort of external hardware for him. When our mother isn't there, he asks whoever's nearby, even strangers. If he's offered a glass of water, he'll turn and ask: "Should I drink, or not?" It's the same with every action. In fact, when my mother and I talk for too long, or if I come for a visit and we have an engrossing conversation, he gets uncomfortable and soon comes over to ask something.

"Mom, Mom . . . Mom, should I go to the bathroom? Mom, should I change my shirt? Mom, should I have a snack?" If the conversation is over the phone, for some unknown reason, it unsettles him more. Perhaps because he doesn't know who the interlocutor absorbing his mother's attention is. Then he interrupts several times after five minutes have passed. If I'm there and I keep our mother occupied for a while, he stares at us with his deep, elongated eyes, dark blue with white edging around the pupils, and says:

"Mom, Mom, should I button these ones?" (He points to the collar of his polo shirt.) "And put on my watch . . . should

I, Mom?" This demand for attention to his needs and his decisions is likely the best survival tool that he's developed. On the other hand, there are decisions that aren't routine. Those that depend on the circumstances of fate and are difficult for another person to control are the most delicate. For example, if you're cold, put on a jumper, or if it's very sunny, take off your jacket. This leads him to catch colds often, because we don't always have someone beside us to remind us of these things and who knows how we are feeling, temperature-wise. The same thing happens when we go to the beach. He will often sit, looking at the sea, his eyes squinting from too much sun, and if we don't put sunscreen and a hat on him he'll burn. It happens sometimes, because my mother, who loves the beach, sometimes forgets.

I think that when M stares at me and her while we talk, he doesn't even realize that he's demanding attention and that perhaps he is feeling some sort of jealousy. When we aren't there, and he doesn't have anyone to ask things to, he must feel as disoriented as I do each time I've had a breakup. Because as happens with love, his center isn't entirely inside him, but rather a part of it is outside of him, in others.

This year we chose the apartment well: it's small but nicely laid out and modern. It has a large terrace overlooking the coastal town. Our bedroom has bunk beds. In this country, apartments are not often designed to house various adults living together, and the layout is usually a large master bedroom and one or two small rooms for the kids. I get the upper bunk, to make things easier for my brother. It's hot, but the sea air makes the night pleasant.

At nine in the morning M's head is in front of mine when I open my eyes.

"Did you sleep well?"

"Yes, M, I slept well." And he smiles.

One these days at the beach when we leave our routines behind, M is a bit more lively and seems encouraged to talk of his own volition, something that doesn't usually happen except when it's a question related to whether he has to carry out one of his basic needs. Sometimes I try to imagine how he perceives me, and if he loves me. I mean, would he suffer if I died, or something serious happened to me? Because there have been times when I was curled up in a ball on the sofa, crying, and he would sit in the armchair beside me, watching TV without even turning his head. He has never called me, either. In fact, he doesn't know how to use a mobile phone, and he doesn't own one. If he did, he'd take so long thinking about whether he should answer, that it would be impossible to get in touch with him anyway. Where would all the energy our family invests in him go if he didn't exist, or if he were, as they say, "normal"? What would our mother have done, and what would she be like? And what would he be like? Maybe a good athlete, and funny like our father, but more studious and introspective like our mother. She says that M would be an artist.

Perhaps, my parents might not even have separated . . . but I think it probably would have happened anyway because they met so young and they're too different. Maybe he and I would have been able to support each other through it.

M likes to do paint-by-numbers books. He had a keychain collection when he was little and not yet so stuck, because time has taken its toll – although we were never explicitly told that his case entailed a cognitive downturn – and he has gradually got frozen over time, more and more so. When he was little he liked atlases of the human body, playing at drawing cuts and stitches on our arms in ballpoint pen. We would also shake hands, when I stuck mine out through the bars of my crib, and we would intone a repetitive song: *Heythereheythereheythereheythereheythere.*

Another game he had was drawing in the air. I remember him often drawing in the air. Not anymore. In fact he no longer has many active interests, but he takes an interest in things around him that others might not perceive in the same way. Once I showed him a magazine with almost nude models in it, with certain parts of their bodies covered by fur coats; he smiled and pointed to the fox head that hung from one of those coats, very close to a generous décolletage.

"Look, a fox," he said.

One of the few things my brother can talk about of his own initiative, apart from asking what he has to do, is announcing that an airplane passed by, or that he saw a lizard on the wall. Or that a passing car has a friend or family member's number plate. Those things are important to him, news that he has to announce to the group. If he's very happy, he will count all the passing planes, and at some unexpected moment he'll say:

"Twenty-three planes have passed by."

M's extraordinary need for attention predates my arrival in the world – ever since I can remember, my mother spent summers giving him extra classes. It manifested in me as a precocious display of independence that involved dressing and acting like a boy. As early as daycare I refused to wear skirts and, when I could, I would pee standing up. Since long hair, braids or other types of extra attention weren't possible for me, I eliminated that from my catalogue of desires and turned them into something deplorable. I felt a certain disdain for girls, and I saw them as weak and twee, with their dolls and little dresses. I didn't want dolls, I wanted a Scalextric. They didn't get me a Scalextric, and instead my mother chose a toy kitchen, which I received on Epiphany in tears. So I transformed a certain lack of attention into independence, and maybe over time it became reciprocal, until paradoxically that attitude had a certain parallel with my brother's autism. Because my presence had to be easy, to not cause more headaches. And a thin layer of ice formed between me and the others; that is how the ice entered me.

WHITE

In Spanish cities, once August arrives everyone is over seventy. Snow-covered heads beneath a scorching sun. Summer leads all the children and families to the beach.

My grandfather sits at an outside table at a bar, one the summer seems to have forgotten. His symmetrical and well-shaped face – very attractive years back – features dark skin, immaculately white hair, eyes the color of a pool (a peaceful, shallow blue), and a large smile, almost always present. The backdrop is blocks of apartments from the eighties around an avenue with young trees, where no one walks. A middle-class neighborhood, neither old nor new, with little commerce. Since he left his farmhouse, which was too big for him at eighty, my grandfather lives in a small modern apartment near my mother's house. Even though he's new to the city, he's made a small coterie of friends since he has breakfast and lunch every day at the same place. On the street they greet him: "Mister Miquel!" I've spent the last few of these mid-August days with him. I used to visit him out in the country. Now, I feel at home in his apartment too. Because it's in relationships, and not in places, that we rest. And my grandfather is at peace, and he shares it. When he grows tired of being at home, he goes down and sits on a bench to get some fresh air. While I write on my computer, tempted to go down with him, I think for a moment about the subversiveness of sitting on a bench on the sidewalk to get some air, when you are an adult of working age.

Those days while I'm here, I accompany him in his daily activities, which are basically: go down to the bar for breakfast, go back there for lunch, and shop for a few essentials. On weekends that routine changes because his favorite bar closes, and he has to go to another bar, where he is also known and has friends. On these short excursions through my childhood haunts on my grandfather's arm, I re-encounter neighbors and former high school classmates, who perhaps find me easier to approach with my amiable companion. They ask me how it's going, what I'm doing for work – hard to explain – and they tell me about their children and grandkids, if they have them. Over the years I've learned that my distracted and often highly focused stance can be taken for lack of interest. While we have our espresso with milk and croissants, my grandfather points to an approaching man: "He's always dressed in black," he says. The man's about seventy, completely bald and wears sunglasses the same color as his clothes. My grandfather introduces us (his name is Miguel, the Spanish equivalent of my grandfather's Catalan name), and invites him to sit down. The man explains how he came to live in this provincial city from his native Múrcia.

"I was an orphan, you know. We were four brothers and sisters and when I turned eighteen I enlisted in the army. When I was about to become a corporal, my aunt wrote and told me to come to Catalonia. My superior officer was Catalan and he supported me, so I left the army and came here. I made the right choice," he says with a smile. "I made the right choice."

A few months ago, he explains, his twenty-five-year-old son died. He was a football player, and he got one of those heart attacks that sometimes take out young athletes. He had fainted and been admitted to the hospital, but neither the team nor the young man let the family know.

"He was very reserved, like my wife . . . The team didn't tell us anything either," he adds with a tinge of stoic resentment. I can see that this man's life is marked by the early deaths of his closest family members.

The man in black gets up from the table and bids us farewell.

"I'm very pleased to meet you. You have a grandfather worth his weight in gold."

And he leaves smiling to greet another of the wintry white heads at the bar's outdoor tables. Hearing his story makes me think that my grandfather has been lucky in many ways. And even so, his wife's illness when his three children were still small projected long shadows over the next two generations. An illness that incapacitated my grandmother shortly after she had the children, which surely froze the sibling relationships. It's certainly true that the three of them have always been distant. Seeing only the light can sometimes mean that we don't see the shadows, and we don't fix the underlying problem. Perhaps that's why my grandfather made it to ninety in such good shape; normally he only looks at the positive side of situations. White things. The black ones are harder to explain. I've always preferred the shades of gray.

AUDITING

What makes talking about family so touchy is that, on one hand, you can't make generalizations, and at the same time there are hardly any social criteria establishing what's fair and what isn't in each home. Close observation of various generations of dysfunctional families – most are in one way or another – while part of one, has allowed me to corroborate the famous beginning of *Anna Karenina*, that all happy families are alike and every unhappy family is unhappy in its own way. One more reason for its members to be orphaned, unable to even take shelter beneath the banner of a common cause, the way they can with public issues. The question is very simple: if someone on the street insults or robs us, it's easy to take legal action. If that same thing, often in much more subtle variations, happens at home, it's more complicated. The laws of each family are created within it, and are practically devoid of external judgments – except for serious cases such as homicide, violence, and sexual abuse. This "law," which generates a certain lack of protection against injustice, is usually written off as family patterns. Therefore, the unequal distribution of emotional and economic resources (which are often impossible to "carve up" equally) of expectations and demands, and also of the enforcement or not of norms (linked to random circumstances such as the gender of the infant or birth order) usually go unpunished, and in the best case scenario, are left to be resolved among siblings. There are no external auditors in families. Those who are lucky have allies. These alliances are usually formed through equally random criteria that have little to do with "justice," like the fact of having siblings, the number of aunts and uncles, cousins, whether there are grandparents, etc. If there hasn't been bad luck, or if it has attacked only one flank, it's likely that a hard core forms, but if it's attacked various sides, the family members may be scattered by the centrifugal force of the explosion, and too busy trying to survive, alone, despite blood ties. Often in those cases, some accuse others of being selfish; they don't realize they are paupers asking each other for charity.

If there is an internal conflict – which is not incompatible with the previous case, since an infinite number of problems can superimpose themselves and we could even say that some attract others – it's likely that the other members take the side of the head of the family in order to retain their protection or avoid disintegration, independently of the real criteria. So many families are supported on the foundations of the unsaid. And in so many the emperor dines each evening, sitting at the table wearing no clothes. Because the day the secret is spoken, we can no longer look each other in the eye. Publicly denouncing abuse within the family can make the denouncer an exile in their own country. Especially in a Mediterranean country where family is the last support in the face of weak government institutions unable to guarantee social justice.

An extreme case is depicted in the film *Festen* (Thomas Vinterberg, 1998). The first from the Dogme 95 movement, this picture portrays a celebration of the family patriarch's birthday. The protagonist, one of his adult children, reveals a family secret in front of the entire clan during the party: the sexual abuses inflicted on him and his twin sister by their father when they were small. The sister recently committed suicide in the hotel run by the family. Despite the initial denial from the other family members during the revelation, there is physical evidence: the note left by his sister before her death. The reactions of various relatives denying the facts, which were known (but not recognized and accepted) by the mother and another sister, make clear that dressing the emperor requires the complicity of the audience. The final revelation becomes a familial catharsis of collective undressing and expulsion of the father. Extreme cases are always easier to identify, but reality is complex, and abuse is often not so clear. What happens if the problem is a continued ducking of responsibilities? How many suicides are actually murders? To whom can an adult turn to denounce years of negligence in her upbringing without being labeled as "immature," "selfish," or "ungrateful"? And, given the impossibility of mending the deficit – which will probably never be acknowledged, and even if it has been, those to blame weren't able to see it at the time or give back what is being demanded – how does one face up to the consequences of that negligence? And what can we call the pressure inflicted on so many mothers who've had to raise kids alone – when it should be a shared task of both parents – without using the word *violence*?

The complexity of responding to these questions proves once more the difficulty of applying the concept of justice that, once across the threshold of the home, becomes extremely problematic. The difference here from the clearer cases explained earlier lies in the fact that, when dealing with passive violence and negligence, the pieces of evidence are omissions. We need a frame of reference in order to know what those omissions are. While, luckily, there are no longer institutions devoted to determining "familial normality," it would be useful if there were some guidelines, at least in terms of the "functionality" of a family, which boils down to giving affection and offering sustenance. Just as one needs a license to drive, I think we all can agree that a parenting license, with a code of good conduct in situations of crisis, would do the world a lot of good.

And if years later you hear expressions like "you have to close that chapter" and "the past is past, look toward the future," you will recognize those who actively or passively were complicit in the injustice – they often have also suffered it; many people will be made "uncomfortable" by what you're saying. We are all familiar with those expressions in this country of revisionist phobias and cadavers in ditches. They mean that the statute of limitations has passed on your case. Because you must forget, smile in gratitude, and accept the laws of the patriarchy. But you should read the pages before you close the chapter.

ULTIMA THULE[16]

Images always precede thought by many years, and they often contain the answer to enigmas. Before I knew what this project would become, one of the first images I gathered for my research was Roni Horn's map of Iceland with the spiral. Now this place touching the Arctic Circle is emerging as the final point of a journey that has included several exhibitions but that is, in essence, narrative.

I started out with a historical investigation into the place of early-twentieth-century polar explorers in the collective imagination, thinking that I was working on a doctoral thesis, until I realized that what I was interested in was actually the enigma of my fascination with those images, images that came back to me with queries about my own identity and posed questions that always converged in those polar documents. From here on out, the exploration had to be interior, I had to go inside

[16] In Roman and Medieval geography, "ultima Thule" designated any place beyond the borders of the known world, and was located in the far north. In Greek mythology Thule was the capital of Hyperborea, the land of the gods. During the Middle Ages, Iceland was sometimes called by this name.

myself to find the origin of those glaciers and thick ice caps. As I perforated the layers of ice, I reached the prime origin of us all, the family. From that point on, the historical research began to seem like a distraction, the creation of images began to seem ambiguous, and the introspection, inadequate.

My new explorations shifted foundations and shook some of my load-bearing walls in a personal deconstruction that left me fragile for months. A process that, along with the illumination of previously hidden areas, has meant the loss of some points of support that I believed were important to my life. All this with the backdrop of a family in a permanent state of reconstruction.

Iceland awaits me: located between the two faults of the European and American continents, with constant volcanic activity, geysers, ice, lava fields: elements that I relate to some areas of my family landscape. Given that this island is the link between the two continents, I relate its geography to the role that we all take on as a result of the union of two different identities. And I declare myself Icelandic, from now on. Putting an end to a process that was never meant to be permanent, but rather just a phase of my journey, I finally face up to – not in books but physically – the region that has occupied my imagination in recent years.

The polar world, like the tropics, is always utopian, by convention and mythology. This voyage is not intended to be epic or exotic, nor is it meant as a means of evasion. Quite the contrary: it is a very intimate journey that I undertake alone to the volcano that leads to the center of the Earth, in order to bring a series of metaphors face-to-face with reality. And as Professor Lidenbrock recommended to his disciple Axel, I will head to the Snæfellsnes peninsula and to the very mouth of Snæfellsjökull to learn a lesson from the abyss. After that, I hope, will come the Stromboli sun.

III

ICELAND, INNER GEOLOGY

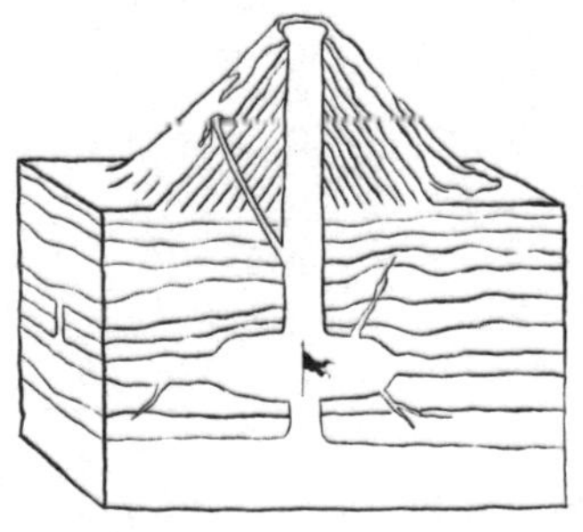

LOST LUGGAGE

I arrive at Keflavík airport in the early morning on August 25. My luggage lost. I was expecting the midnight sun but I find a black, cold, windy night. I have the bus all to myself, and it drops me at some indeterminate point on the coastal highway. Only the street number confirms the door in the dark gray building is for the hostel. The nightshift receptionist gives me a card to get into the shared room. When I open the door off the long hallway, there are boys' heads sleeping in bunks and the smell of sweat. I turn tail and ask for the girls' room I'd reserved. That's more like it. Maybe tomorrow I'll get my luggage. Good night.

Four hours later I'm awoken by the moving of bags and the opening and closing of doors. At nine I have no choice but to get up. I explore the place a little, which, for a hostel, has kind of nice decoration. Nordic design with historic details and old atlases. No word on my luggage yet. At reception they tell me that the Blue Lagoon thermal baths rent bathing costumes. Floating in hot water is the only thing I can stand doing today. I take the bus. We pass through cracked, moss-covered lava fields. Small, voluptuous ripples. A golf course sneaks into the landscape for a second. I'm on Mars. The blue lagoon emerges from the dunes. It's a space station surrounded by fluorescent blue tongues of water. Inside hides a perfectly orchestrated tourist complex. Outside, gray sky and discreet cold. The water is calming: 38°C of azure blue and healing white mud. People float in the lunar landscape like statues made of chalk.

I decide to take my lost luggage as a sign: no rucksacks on this trip. Like everyone else, I paint myself white and float. Noting the efficiency of the organization and transportation, on the way back to the hostel I think that it's much easier to get to the Arctic than to reach certain areas of one's self. On the bus I feel new, weightless. The older, married couple in the back spends the trip arguing. They don't raise their voices but their words exude a certain bitterness. Why do we suffer so much? Because we want things that others aren't giving us. Because of the self-deception that often ends up involving others. Because we don't know what we want or we don't know how to communicate it. Because of the accumulated, unpaid debts over the years. Right now I appreciate traveling alone.

At night, the hostel's common space is lively. The tourists, most of them young, mix with the local population, which comes to see concerts there. Today a Polish jazz band is playing. I'd like to put on more appropriate clothing but my luggage is still lost. I'm wearing hiking shoes because they took up too much space in the suitcase I checked. Now I realize that wearing shoes that aren't my style makes me feel insecure; I feel decoded as an American tourist. The young Icelanders are original and interpret fashion in their own way. Unlike in Mediterranean countries, the older folks do too. It seems that here being different isn't just something for the young or for outsiders. It's even cultivated. After the concert I decide to go out and look for a restaurant that was recommended to me for its lobster soup. I head up the coastal highway toward the old port. From what I can see, Reykjavík is small; I go around the city in fifteen minutes. There's a line outside the recommended restaurant, Sægreifinn. The place is tiny like a fishing shack, and the diners sit tall on benches. The ceiling is low, with wooden beams painted white. Like many seafood restaurants, it is decorated with nets, fishing tools, portraits of the founders. There is a small taxidermied seal among the nets on the wall. The seal's glass eyes are almost poignant. Once I'm seated at one of the benches, I see a picture of a waterfall in front of me that looks like it was done with finger paint. It would be kitschy if it were technically well painted, but as it is, it has a naïf air to it. Another small picture depicts an erupting volcano in cross-stitch. The technique makes the scene homey, even cozy. The soup is very spicy, with big pieces of lobster. I finish it off happily.

THE GOLDEN CIRCLE

Organized daytrip. The bus leaves at eight in the morning. The guide, a skinny, perky Icelandic woman about sixty years old, picks up the loudspeaker, introduces herself and after a couple of sarcastic jokes to break the ice she starts in with the information: “Iceland is located between two tectonic plates, the American continent and the European one. The plates move because of continental drift, causing the central fault to separate approximately two and a half centimeters each year . . . The Snæfellsjökull volcano, which according to Verne is the entrance to the center of the Earth, is active and is expected to erupt again in the next two hundred and fifty years . . . The energy that creates the friction of the plates is the one that creates the geothermal energy that supplies the island . . .” That makes me think that one can extract energy from an unstable area. Like the perpetual need to construct meaning in those of us who find themselves in constant friction with the world. I continue taking notes: “The type of rock that surrounds the island was created by the earth’s contact with the ice. It is a soft, young rock that can’t be built upon. Between the continents’ two tectonic plates, we will visit the fault that separates them in the valley of Thingvallavatn. This valley gets its name from *Thing* (assembly) and *vellir* (valley or field), where Icelanders established one of the first parliaments in the world. The valley's lake, which has widened some seventy meters in the last 1,000 years due to the separation of the plates, has a few small islands in it." They are no man's land, they don't belong to either continent.

Given that more than half of Iceland is glacial, this country is dripping with cascades. We stop at the imposing waterfalls at Gullfoss ("Golden Falls"), located on the wide ravine of the Hvitá River. Its energy and ferocity combined with the purifying power of the water exert a magnetic pull on me that I can't quite rationalize.

Helga (I'll call her Helga) explains a legend to us: once upon a time there was a girl who worked on a farm and had a reputation as a good healer. One day, while she was hanging up the clothes, she sensed a presence behind her, but she had heard many legends about elves and knew not to look them in the eyes or speak to them, or something terrible would happen to her. So she continued hanging up the clothes as if she'd noticed nothing. The being, who looked very friendly, came closer and asked her if she would come with him. She continued as if nothing had happened. Finally the being promised her that if she followed him he would bring her back home unharmed, and that she would never regret it. Everyone knows that you can only agree to follow an elf or troll if they first promise to return you safe and sound to the world of humans. Finally the girl accepted and followed him. They arrived at a very lovely farm and, when they entered, the elf led her to a large room where an elf woman seemed to be struggling for her life with a difficult birth. The girl rolled up her sleeves, asked for the tools she needed and successfully assisted the birth. The elf thanked her and took her back to her own farm. In her bedroom the girl found a beautiful dress, with embroidery so delicate there was no way it could have been made by human hands. She later married and had a family, and her daughter inherited the gift of healing. That is the only way you should accept gifts from magical beings: as compensation for a favor or a job, and never right off, since otherwise you would attract disaster. That reminds me of my earlier reflections on the kinds of gift, and adds a new perspective. What is the meaning of all those warnings about gifts from supernatural creatures? Are they tied to cautiousness in dealing with strangers or those who are different?

Being that it's the third day, and I've stuck to my plans despite having no luggage, I think the only real problem that you can have these days when traveling (except for those related to safety and ID) is not having money. Iceland doesn't have crime issues, so unless you make the mistake of stepping into a geyser, the rest can be solved if you have credit on your card. Any equipment that you've forgotten, or that's stuck in your lost luggage, can be rented. If you're willing to pay, there are organized trips to any glacier, volcano, fjord or remote lava camp that you want to visit, either on foot, horseback, by Jeep, car or boat. That's life, after all. The adventure begins when the money runs out.

*

Almost all of the rooms in the hostel are shared, with three or four sets of bunk beds. They are separated by gender in most cases. It is the cheapest I could find that wasn't camping, even though it's very dear compared to Spanish prices. In my room there are a couple of young Israeli women in their twenties, a Canadian my age who came to run a marathon, and a twenty-year-old American:

"Hey, how are you? What's your name? You want some? They're delicious!"

Without waiting for a response to her three questions, she holds out a cone of fries with ketchup and mayonnaise.

"No, thanks. Where do you come from?"

"L.A." she says with the characteristic nasal voice. "My name is A. I'm going to London but I wanted to visit some European cities first."

She has the face and hair of a doll, with the body you'd expect from the amount of fries she was scarfing down. She was doing her European tour before starting an internship at a British law firm.

"I'm very ambitious."

She adds me on her social networks and I ask her where her last name comes from. It's Polish. One of her grandmothers was in a Nazi concentration camp "or something like that." Hearing her talk about it, the Holocaust sounded like an old family feud.

I go to have dinner and when I get back, A is at the computer with a bottle of beer in her hand. She goes out into the hallway in her pajamas to ask for help opening it and she comes back with a group of Danes who say we should go out with them. They're meeting some Icelandic friends at a pub in the city. I sign on out of pure ethnological curiosity. There we end up dancing to Taylor Swift songs, which Danes, Americans, and Icelanders all seem to know by heart. To hell with exoticism. I try to talk to one guy who seems like the oldest, in his late twenties, who can't take his eyes off of A. He distractedly tells me that he studies Literary Theory, that in Denmark the government pays them a modest salary for studying. Our brief conversation over, he pounces on A, giggling and putting on a nasal voice. I go out onto the dance floor. The other Danes interpret that as some sort of flirting and one of them who looks like Barbie's boyfriend Ken clings to me and keeps spinning me around and around. I get away by heading to the bar for a drink and ten minutes later I see he's snogging an Icelandic woman, one of the very few unattractive ones I've seen. A, the American, is leaving early the next day for Amsterdam; she will spend two days in each city on her European tour. The literary Dane takes her to the airport, stopping on the way for fries. In the days that follow I see A on the web, posting photos of her stop in each European city in a folder entitled "Eurotrash."

THURSDAY, AUGUST 27
JÖKULLSÁRLÓN NATIONAL PARK

LICORICE

In Iceland's black earth the licorice plant grows in abundance. Nature is coherent.

ERUPTIONS

After a volcanic eruption the earth is left covered in ash. The ash has minerals that fertilize the soil and nourish the plants: the disaster brings good harvests.

WATERFALLS

They are protected by the pressure, in the form of wind, exerted by the water as it falls. There is no need to put up safety barriers: they themselves keep us out of danger.

ICELAND

Black fungus between two tiles. On a human scale: hyperlandscape.

SHEEP

It doesn't matter how tall the mountain is: Icelandic sheep, their wool puffed up like popcorn, graze motionless at every height as if they had flown up there.

JÖKULLSÁRLÓN

On the wide deltas of black sand that lead into the sea, all the sadness of humanity.

GLACIERS

Glaciers, like volcanoes, also awaken. When they do, they drag off everything in their path: bridges, highways . . . Icelanders are used to starting over.

ICE LIGHT

The light inside icebergs is impossible to capture on film.

AURORAS

According to Scandinavian folklore, an aurora borealis is the spirit of a woman who has never married. Seems like a good outcome to me.

FRIDAY, AUGUST 28

A visit to the Reykjavík Art Museum. There is a Richard Serra exhibition, about the site-specific piece he made in Áfangar, a small Icelandic town. In the video-interview, the artist highlights something about this country that has made an impact on me in the last few days: the predominance of geological time over historical time.

The influence of scale is highly relevant both in works of art and in landscape. Mountains are absolutely dependent on this factor; without it, they are nothing more than a pile of sand. A sign, on the other hand, never loses its power, no matter how small. That is why I'm more interested in words than in sculptures. A *yes* is always a *yes* and doesn't lose its value based on where it is written, or at what scale, nor when whispered or shouted.

I spend some time at the museum bookstore. Museum bookstores are my favorite places in the world after libraries. I search for a book about Icelandic artists. What relationship do they have to this nature that surrounds them? My eye is drawn to the image of an artist's performance in a catalogue of local art. The photograph shows a rainbow (very common on the island due to the profusion of waterfalls) made of fabric, which the artist has set aflame. This environment of infinite winters and omnipresent waterfalls, over the years, must exert some sort of despotic absolutism. The options: 1) romanticism moldered by dampness, 2) the most common: becoming a musician, 3) fire, destruction.

After that visit I head to a public pool that the receptionist recommended. He assured me that it's his favorite, and not many people know about it. It's on the outskirts of the city, in a neighborhood of single-family homes. Even though it's late August, the icy wind makes my walk through the Reykjavík suburbs feel long. I think I'm getting a sore throat. Why did I wear jeans with holes in them on the flight? Fashion is absurd but without it the world would be monotonous. The cold air enters through the holes in my pants. After walking in circles without finding the place, or a single pedestrian, I go into a bar to ask. Inside, it teems with life: young couples, children, and the scent of freshly baked cake. "Where can I find the Vesturbæjarlaug?" Across the street. And the waitress points to a gray wall with no signage. At the entrance to the pools, the receptionist, a young blond woman with elongated blue eyes and a very stiff pageboy hairdo, gives me the pertinent explanations in a monotone voice, scarcely gesticulating. I go into the changing rooms. Outside, the thermometer reads 9°C but the wind chill makes it seem like zero. The risk isn't outside of the city, but in it; there is no indoor pool. I hurry in bikini to the busiest pool, which is 38°C. There is an area a few feet deep where people stretch out to sunbathe. Alternatively, you can sit in a pool with bubbles, or another one without bubbles. I decide that I like this activity, no need to do anything. There is no one in the swimming lanes. I can understand why. Soon the pool has completely warmed me up. Around me, tattooed Viking families play with laughing white babies. Here people have children in a relaxed way and seem to enjoy them at every age, unlike Southern Europe, where having a family when you're part of the new hand-to-mouth middle class is an operation that requires strategy if you want certain guarantees.

In the Jacuzzi area, a man of about sixty comes over to me out of curiosity. He asks me where I'm from and what my name is. The younger men watch out of the corner of their eyes and smile. I wonder if he does this all the time, and I play along. He tells me his name is Bragi (he pronounces the B like a P). "Praguiíí?" I repeat. "It's the name of the Norse god of poetry," he replies. I ask him if he's from there. "Yes, from the pool," he says sarcastically. The pool is located on the site of ancient thermal baths, very close to the first colonists' settlements. He says he writes poetry, that he's published a volume.

"Can I find it in the bookstores?" "No, only in the library, it's out of print. But if you want we can meet up one day and I'll bring you a copy." Getting together with an older guy to talk about anthroposophy on a Friday night isn't terribly appealing. I dodge the offer. I emerge from the pool radiant. The next day there is no trace of my sore throat. I tend to think that Bragi wasn't lying to me in the slightest: he's lived there, in the thermal waters, since the first colonists brought their pagan gods.

SATURDAY, AUGUST 29

SNÆFELLSNES PENINSULA

Organized excursion. We leave the capital in a small bus. It seems there won't be a guide, rather that the driver will explain a few things to us. He raises his tone of voice to give us the first bit of information: "Sixty percent of the island's surface is glacial." The people in the back can't hear him. When he drives off he leaves the bus door open. He switches speakers. It still doesn't work. Discouraged, he stops explaining and submerges under a deep silence. My eyes follow the mossy waves of the lava fields. We reach the coastal highway that edges the peninsula. Gradually the peak of Snæfellsjökull comes into focus, with its white tip illuminated by the sun. It is one of the tallest on the island, its crater crowned by the glacier that can be seen from a distance on a clear day. The peak split when, 1,750 years ago, the volcano beneath the glacier erupted and it melted inside the magma chamber itself, creating a huge cauldron that is now filled with ice. I find the mix of fire and ice involved in the formation of that still active volcano fascinating. On the ground near the streams, like something out of a dream, white swans appear amid the black lava. The swans will soon constitute a plague on the island. According to the guidebook I end up consulting to find out more, there are those who believe that this area is one of the Earth's seven energy points or chakras. We stop at the Djúpalónssandur beach, about four kilometers from the volcano's slope, which offers magnificent views of the peak. Once we are out of the bus, Oskar, the driver/guide, explains that the round pebbles found on this beach hold the energy of the place. He whispers to me that I should take a few. There are still the metal remains of the wreck of the *Epine*, a British trawler that went down in 1948, drowning fourteen of its crew of nineteen. On the beach, the sea, black and calm, has internal currents that can quickly pull you away from the shore. The mountainous formations on the horizon, not very tall and covered in splotches of snow, make me think of orcas moving through the Arctic.

The bus stops near the summit and we are taken to a cave entrance where we're introduced to the guide for the next stretch of our journey, this time vertical, into the bowels of the volcano. I think of the description of Hans Bjelke in *Journey to the Center of the Earth*: "a tall man, of robust build. This fine fellow must have been possessed of great strength. His eyes, set in a large and ingenuous face, seemed to me very intelligent; they were of a dreamy sea-blue."[17] The young man gives us helmets and a torch

[17] Translation by Frederick Amadeus Malleson.

and our small group starts a descent into the lava cave. The black hole is covered in stalagmites and dripping stalactites, brown layers of rust overlap with the lava and mineral formations. Lilac iridescence from magnesium, yellow layers of sulfur.

Above us, tiny shining spots illuminate the darkness. They are bacteria that feed on the dripping water. A vast city seen from an airplane is now the ceiling. Near a spiral staircase that leads to dark, invisible depths, a sign points downward: *Stromboli, 8,500 km >*. We descend another thirty meters. Absolute blackness and silence. I remember the enigmatic quote from Arne Saknussemm: "Descend, bold traveler, into the crater of the jökull of Sneffels, which the shadow of Scartaris touches before the calends of July, and you will attain the center of the earth; which I have done." Here we stop our descent. We turn off the torches. Total silence. Complete blackness. Cold and damp. The guide starts singing a happy song, one of the ones shepherds sing as they return home through the frozen, dark Icelandic winter. He asks us to clap along.

> If you're happy and you know it clap your hands . . . If you're happy and you know it clap your hands . . . If you're happy and you know it, then your face will surely show it, if you're happy and you know it, clap your hands.

Singing in the dark is my lesson from the abyss.

Hans accompanies us out into the light again, and we climb the spiral staircase that leads us to the mouth of the cave. Traveling nowadays requires very little bravery. Oskar is waiting for us in the bus. He turns over the motor and we head off again with the door open. (Laughter in the background.) This time he tells us, in a louder tone of voice: "If the world was twenty-four hours old, Iceland would have appeared in the last five seconds! That's why there is no hard rock! Volcanic rock is soft! They say that the name Iceland was some sort of anti-marketing scheme to discourage possible non-Danish colonists from coming here! Greenland is actually a land of ice! They gave it that name to encourage people to go there!"

The tourists in the back can't hear a thing. A Swedish man with only one eye finally sits up beside the driver and plugs in the speaker. With British diction so good he could do voice-overs, he begins a dissertation on the origin of the name of the Snæfellsnes Peninsula. (More laughter.) The driver seems to have sunk into his seat. The Swede continues: "*Snæ* comes from 'snow,' *fells* from 'fall.' So the peninsula is called 'Place where snow falls' . . . " Resigned, Oskar takes us back to the capital. In the pocket of my coat, I fondle the little black pebbles from the Djúpalónssandur beach. They exude warmth.

Back at the hotel, they tell me that my luggage has arrived.

Concert in the common space at the hostel. Apparat Organ Quartet, a local group that promises to get us dancing. I go down with one of my roommates. She's from Alaska, about twenty years old with long blond hair. The Icelanders are lined up at the door. It is sold out, even for those of us who are guests at the hostel. We think to try the back door, which leads to the courtyard, and we manage to get in. While the musicians play, the Alaskan takes selfies with her iPad and makes a face as if she were looking at a very cute baby. She retransmits the evening to her eight hundred Snapchat "friends" and pays no attention to me. In the end I decide to ignore her too. The concert is really fun.

SUNDAY, AUGUST 30

After five days in Reykjavík waiting for my suitcase, I decide to take a shortcut and go straight to Akureyri, the largest city in the north, on a domestic flight. The city's airport is one of the smallest I've ever seen. The tiny plane is definitely a "light" aircraft. The flight takes forty minutes and saves me six hours on the bus that, after the luggage delay, I can't afford to waste. We take off over the coast of Reykjavík. The black color of the water fades into a bright, Caribbean blue in some strips. Is there a tropical paradise beneath the icy water of the fjords?

MONDAY, AUGUST 31

The tiny island of Grímsey is the northernmost point in Iceland. Forty-one kilometers from the coast of Akureyri, it's the only part of the country located inside the Arctic Circle. Despite the warnings against tourists visiting the place, I head to the small coastal town of Dreyvik to catch the ferry. The three-hour trip has a bad reputation because of the groundswell; some ships have had to turn back halfway with all of the crew nauseous. Once we leave the port, in the passengers' cabin they show an ethnographic documentary about the island . . . *Puffin egg hunters on the cliffs . . . Before there was machinery to do so, the entire town helped pull the climbers from the abyss onto terra firma with their valuable treasure* . . . "The abysses contain treasures . . . others help us out of them," I write down . . . *The last polar bear came to the island floating on an iceberg from the Arctic in 1969 . . . They usually ended up attacking people's pets and had to be shot . . . Some winters they could walk to Iceland from the island on the layer of ice that formed on the sea* . . . While I'm writing I start to feel poorly and run out onto the deck. I laboriously vomit my breakfast overboard while the few tourists who withstood the cold wind on the prow are photographing the backs of distant whales.

After a couple of the worst hours of my life, Grímsey emerges on the horizon. Miraculously, the sky above it is clear. The piece of flat land atop the cliffs that are coming into view has a surface area of some five square kilometers. When we arrive we are greeted by a few fishermen's houses, a small grocery, and a single hostel. On the arctic tundra surface, nothing else stands out. The sky, populated by thousands of different species of birds, is the only part of the island that's truly inhabited. Glaucous gulls and arctic terns are the main species. I get off the ferry with the rest of the tourists, a smallish group: six young American nuns, four women in their sixties who seem to be celebrating something, a couple of French guys with big cameras, and an Icelandic mother and son. After leaving the port the group disperses calmly.

I need some time to recover from my seasickness and I have a hot soup at the hostel bar. When I'm feeling up to going out everyone has disappeared on the clear horizon – as with Iceland's mainland, there's not a single tree. Looking at the sea, the Icelandic fjords in the background are imposing. Described as rugged and windy, Grímsey today seems friendly and spring-like, perhaps to compensate for the hardships I endured on the trip there. I take the path through the tundra toward the point marking the polar circle. A few arctic terns fly over me, closer and closer, threatening me in their language. I start to feel like Tippi Hedren in the Hitchcock film. As I find out later, the arctic tern is one of the most aggressive and territorial types of tern. They are the true masters of the place.

I wonder if the legend of Hyperborea, the northernmost land in all of Greek mythology, prompted us to visit Grímsey.

According to René Guénon, Hyperborea is where various esoteric systems believe the earthly and celestial planes converge. Located within the Arctic Circle, it would be the supreme country according to the original meaning of the pole: the pole as the point around which everything revolves, the axis. The Vedic texts call it Avesta, and at different moments in the history of humanity it has been located in different places, all of them close to the North Pole. Often this axis of the world is represented as a sacred mountain. As I mentally review that mythology my eyes follow the nuns as they head toward the post marking where the Arctic Circle passes. Of course everyone knows it doesn't really mark the correct spot; the circle moves about fifteen meters a year and now must be about twenty meters away. Like the post indicating the North Pole, which is mobile because of the ice drift, this post has to be moved periodically. We need points of reference, but reality often doesn't let itself be measured. The need for these references when we are in unknown territory is what, despite how absurd tourism seems in our own hometowns, makes it so easy for us to shift into that role when we are away. By the post there is a small set of stairs with a platform to take a photo of yourself, and various signs indicating the distance in kilometers from the main world capitals. The group of nuns ahead of me are already there. They kindly offer to take my portrait to commemorate the feat. The Icelandic mother and son watch us thoughtfully. They observe us a long time in silence. The French guys arrive later, place a stuffed toy on the commemorative platform, take a photo of it and head off laughing.

Once around the field of tundra and cliffs and I can confirm that, apart from that secular pilgrimage, photographing birds is the only possible activity. I decide to go back to the bar to finish writing the postcards I planned to send from there to prove I'd made it. They collect the mail at the grocery store. While I write postcards at the bar, a man who looks like an Icelander and was on the boat asks me if I saw "the whale" from the ferry.

"I was busy."

"Yes, I saw that," he says smiling.

He explains that he's an anthropologist, doing a thesis on the women of Grímsey Island.

"You see that woman?" he points to the waitress. "She's not from here, she's from Reykjavík. She fell in love with a fisherman and came here to live with him. I met her last year when I arrived. She was very pregnant and was waiting at the port with a big smile on her face. This year the baby is already big and she still has the same smile."

I think about Ingrid Bergman in *Stromboli*, marrying a fisherman to get out of a refugee camp. The couple settles in a town constantly threatened by the volcano – the volcano where Otto Lidenbrock and his nephew Axel appear at the end of *Journey to the Center of the Earth*. Oppressed by a town that rejects her, Bergman (Karin) flees, crossing Stromboli as it erupts. In the end, near the crater, Karin asks God for help. Tired of waiting for a reply, in my story the protagonist enters the bowels of the magma chamber. She navigates seas of lava for days and nights until she emerges from the mouth of Snæfellsjökull. The final image of the film is her hitchhiking amid Icelandic lava fields.

K, emerging from Snæfellsjökull.

On the way back, the ferry advances motionlessly and we reach the Dreyvik port without any queasiness. They told me there's a bus to Akureyri from the port, but all I find there is a man waiting in front of a car. He is the bus driver. From what he tells me, since he only had two people to pick up, he brought his regular car. The other passenger is a young woman who's been hitchhiking across the island. I wonder what her story is and whether she's emerged from the volcano.

The day ends with fish soup with touches of curry, and a dish of *pokkari*, a cod and potato stew that's typical of the region.

What was my pilgrimage? Unable to answer my own question, I sleep heavily and peacefully. The next day I remember that there was not a single moment of nostalgia, there, at the end of the inhabited world.

TUESDAY, SEPTEMBER 1

The last day of my trip. The buses have shifted from summer to winter schedules, and everything is less frequent. I just missed the only bus that goes to the Myváth lake region, where the Goðafoss waterfalls are located. In the tourist office they tell me that the only alternative is hitchhiking. I head to the petrol station on the outskirts of town, where they make me a cardboard sign with the name of my destination as if it were a regular thing. I wait for five minutes on the side of the highway and a light truck soon stops. A man about forty with reddish hair and weathered skin timidly invites me in. He says that he can take me about twenty-five kilometers. I get in repeating in my head what I've read: the island is very safe, there is no crime, and it's very normal to hitchhike. Ingolfur explains that they've just started collecting the sheep that are scattered over the mountain, to put them in their winter shelters. They often do this on horseback. "And what if you don't find them all?" "Then we try again, at least three more times. Last year nineteen were lost and we were able to recover them in December. With their thick skin they can last just fine." "And don't they have predators?" He shakes his head, keeping his eyes on the road. "What about the arctic fox?" "It'd have to be a very weak little lamb."

We part with a handshake and I go back to waiting by the side of the highway with the sign in my hand. A jeep stops in front of me after five minutes. Stefan, who works building tunnels to Norway, is from this region. We pass by the farm where he grew up. It's isolated between the typical low mountains and lava fields. He is looking for a picture on his mobile as he drives and we drift onto the other side of the two-lane highway. "Watch out!" He corrects our direction and passes me the mobile, smiling: "This is my superjeep." On the screen is a red car with giant wheels, atop a white summit. Stefan drops me right near the magnificent Goðafoss waterfalls and I'm relieved to get out. The falls are about forty meters wide, an imposing torrent. A sign reads: "The Waterfalls of the Gods." During the island's Christianization at the turn of the first millennium, spiritual leader Thorgeir Ljosvetningagodi threw the wooden icons of the last pagan gods into the falls after spending a day and a night meditating under a blanket of fur. Tourists dressed with colorful mackintoshes respectfully approach from both sides of the falls.

That night:

The Goðafoss waterfalls enter through your eye sockets and drag all the bones of your skeleton downriver to the volcano. After a couple of eruptions smash the magma chamber, water stagnates, forming a glacier. The crater is brimming with snow. Its eruption regurgitates tabular icebergs that descend along the flanks, crashing into each other with the loud dull sounds of an avalanche.

Arriving at the mouth of the river, ancient hands, pointing to the last pagan gods, melt languidly beneath the August sun. The complicit – opportunists, liars, cowards – watch from the shore, motionless, with Gore-Tex sneakers. After a typical Icelandic winter, their black, porous, petrified bodies fall into the river. The seals ignore them. Some are broken up and polished round by the tide, becoming pebbles. The pebbles end up in the pockets of visitors to the Djúpalónssandur beach. Everyone feels the energy they exude when they hold them, but the warmth they give off is nothing more than rage and impotence over being there. The biggest liar of them all ends up hanging in the nets at the Seegreifinn restaurant, famous for its lobster soup. His poignant, childish glass eyes look at the women, in search of compassion.

A puffin egg hunter climbs the crags behind the wall of water at the Seljalandsfoss Falls. Tourists in raincoats grasp her hands and pull her up. Their wet hands slip and she falls off the cliff. The centrifugal pressure of the waterfalls lets her drop gently into the water without hurting herself. Tabular icebergs float on the surface. She grabs a bit of white ice and makes a game of sinking it and letting it re-emerge.

POSTSCRIPT

Brother in ice, I wonder if recreating you here will do us any good. Mom wanted to protect you, by wrapping you in silence. I only make images, fictions, only you know what you've lived through . . . which generally must be good, because you are in good hands. There are some exceptions, like when we were little and a classmate saw you in front of the school, wrapped in tape. Or years later when I realized that bodybuilding freak took advantage of your innocent appearance and made you ask people for money on the street. When I show any indignity here, it's nothing more than other people's. Because you expose the level of humanity of those around you. The smallest things, those that fall on you like a rain of dead leaves and which you've been sweeping up for years on the city's long avenues, that rain that accompanies you after you say goodbye to Mom and head to the day center, jerkily shaking her hand and repeating "Goodbye, I'm off" five times, those "Hurry up, aren't you ready yet?" and those "Out of the way" that form a lake of orders and reproaches, of which one can only see the surface – everyone has their own life, mine has to keep on keeping on too. And because deep down no one knows anything about your secret life; I don't have the power of an omniscient narrator, I am just a partial observer who intuits that those are the things that have made you submerge, deeper and deeper each day. Your daily life, apart from that, is brightened at the day center by the attendant and your mates who take care of you; at home, Mom, Granddad, the animals.

There are those who say you're an angel. I don't believe that. I think your life is just another one of the tales told by an idiot that make up this world.

The most basic difference between us is that you are dependent; the weight of that dependence – borne by those around you in various ways, sometimes with work, other times in their awareness, or as isolation – is a measure of each of us, also a measure of the government, whose lack of assistance makes that weight a burden.

On the other hand, this book isn't about your life, which is only yours; it is an exploration; the search for the origin of a voice and gaze of my own, and that is why you appear in it. Because as I insisted on advancing toward the blind spot where everything around me was all white, the point from which I could see nothing and didn't know which way to walk, feeling my way, identifying the origin and direction of the footprints, it was by following that trail that I found the smallest of the set of seven figures who project that voice, the figurine that was not hollow but solid, the matrix that, like *Symzonia*, had given rise to the rest of the shapes and situations:

The six-year-old girl who defended her thirteen-year-old brother in the schoolyard. The girl who was the flip side of the boy in ice, the girl who said:

"I want to see a library!" And her mother took her to a senior center, right before she discovered the public library on her own. Because despite the kids that laughed at the siblings, asking if they were both retards, even though those boys were twice her size, she who still wet the bed, especially when she had that dream where her parents and aunts and uncles are steering huge spiders with controls as if they were spaceships – spiders that years later she recognized in the work of Louise Bourgeois – sometimes, not always but now and then, someone can will the impossible into existence, and because thanks to you, Brother in Ice, I found my voice for the first time.

SELECTED POLAR BIBLIOGRAPHY

Alexander, Caroline, *The Endurance: Shackleton's Legendary Antarctic Expedition*, Knopf, New York, 1998.

Fiennes, Ranulph, *Race to the Pole: Tragedy, Heroism, and Scott's Antarctic Quest*, Hyperion, London, 2004.

Fleming, Fergus, *Ninety Degrees North: The Quest for the North Pole*, Perseus Oto, London, 2003.

Garrard-Cherry, Apsley, *The Worst Journey in the World*, Vintage Classics, New York, 2010.

Onfray, Michel, *Esthétique du Pol Nord*, Photographies d'Alain Szuczuczynski, Editions Grasset, Paris, 2002.

Otis, Laura (ed.), *Literature and Science in the Nineteenth Century*, Oxford World's Classics, Oxford, 2002.

Potter, Russell Alan, *Arctic Spectacles: The Frozen North in Visual Culture, 1818–1875*, University of Washington Press, Washington, 2007.

Rossi, Sergio, *Un viaje a la Antártida*, Tusquets, Barcelona, 2013.

Zweig, Stefan (trans. Anthea Bell), *Shooting Stars: Ten Historical Miniatures*, Pushkin Press, London, 2013.

Cover image: Taken from *Description of a View of the Continent of Boothia*. Henry Courtney Selous, 1835. Collection of Russell A. Potter.

A representation of the search for a northwest passage on the expedition headed by John Ross (1829–1833). The image depicts Ross's adventures chronologically and geographically, trapped for almost four years in the area of the Northwest Passage. One can recognize some of his exploits, like his encounter with the Inuit and the death of two of his crew. The map was the result of a collaboration between the explorer and the painter H.C. Selous.

After writing a heartfelt letter of complaint, the airline I flew to Iceland with compensated me for the temporary loss of my luggage.

I also finished this book and submitted it to a literary contest. I won.

ACKNOWLEDGMENTS

To Antònia Vila, senior professor in the Artistic and Publishing Processes section of the Department of Visual Arts and Design at the Faculty of Fine Arts at the University of Barcelona, who gave me the first polar bibliographic recommendations, and with whom I share white obsessions.

To Celia Rico and Rosa Samper, for being my sounding boards during the writing process.

To my mother, for being there as much as she could.

Dear readers,

As well as relying on bookshop sales, And Other Stories relies on subscriptions from people like you for many of our books, whose stories other publishers often consider too risky to take on.

Our subscribers don't just make the books physically happen. They also help us approach booksellers, because we can demonstrate that our books already have readers and fans. And they give us the security to publish in line with our values, which are collaborative, imaginative and 'shamelessly literary'.

All of our subscribers:

- receive a first-edition copy of each of the books they subscribe to
- are thanked by name at the end of our subscriber-supported books
- receive little extras from us by way of thank you, for example: postcards created by our authors

BECOME A SUBSCRIBER, OR GIVE A SUBSCRIPTION TO A FRIEND

Visit andotherstories.org/subscribe to help make our books happen. You can subscribe to books we're in the process of making. To purchase books we have already published, we urge you to support your local or favourite bookshop and order directly from them – the often unsung heroes of publishing.

OTHER WAYS TO GET INVOLVED

If you'd like to know about upcoming events and reading groups (our foreign-language reading groups help us choose books to publish, for example) you can:

- join the mailing list at: andotherstories.org/join-us
- follow us on Twitter: @andothertweets
- join us on Facebook: facebook.com/AndOtherStoriesBooks
- admire our books on Instagram: @andotherpics
- follow our blog: andotherstoriespublishing.tumblr.com

This book was made possible thanks to the support of:

Amy Benson · Aaron McEnery · Aaron Schneider · Abigail Charlesworth · Ada Gokay · Adam Barnard · Adam Bowman · Adam Lenson · Agata Rucinska · Aifric Ni Chathmhaoil · Aileen-Elizabeth Taylor · Ailsa Peate · Aisling Reina · Ajay Sharma · Alan McMonagle · Alana Marquis-Farncombe · Alasdair Hutchison · Alastair Gillespie · Alastair Laing · Alex Fleming · Alex Hancock · Alex Ramsey · Alexander Bunin · Alexandra Citron · Alexandra de Verseg-Roesch · Alexia Richardson · Alfred Birnbaum · Ali Conway · Ali MacKenzie · Ali Smith · Alice Nightingale · Alice Ramsey · Alison Layland · Alison Lock · Alison MacConnell · Alison Winston · Adele Stripe · Amanda · Amber Da · Amelia Ashton · Amelia Dowe · Amine Hamadache · Amitav Hajra · Andrea Reece · Andrew Marston · Andrew McCallum · Andrew Rego · Andrew Wilkinson · Aneesa Higgins · Angela Everitt · Angharad Jones · Anna-Maria Aurich · Anna Dowrick · Anna Glendenning · Anna Johnson · Anna McKee-Poore · Anna Milsom · Anna Pigott · Anne Carus · Anne Frost · Anne Guest · Anne Ryden · Anne Sanders · Anne Stokes · Anneliese O'Malley · Annie McDermott · Anonymous · Anonymous · Anonymous · Anthony Brown · Anthony McGuinness · Anthony Quinn · Antonia Lloyd-Jones · Antonia Saske · Antonio de Swift · Antony Pearce · Aoife Boyd · Archie Davies · Arne Van Petegem · Arwen Smith · Asako Serizawa · Asher Norris · Audrey Mash · Avril Marren · Barbara & Terry Feller · Barbara Mellor · Barry John Fletcher · Bella Besong · Ben Schofield · Ben Thornton · Benjamin Judge · Beth Hancock · Beth O'Neill · Bettina Rogerson · Beverly Jackson · Bianca Duec · Bianca Jackson · Bianca Winter · Björn Halldórsson · Blythe Ridge Sloan · Brandon Knibbs · Brendan McIntyre · Briallen Hopper · Bridget Gill · Brigid O'Connor · Brigita Ptackova · Caitlin Halpern · Caitlin Liebenberg · Caitriona Lally · Callie Steven · Cameron Lindo · Caren Harple · Carl Emery · Carla Carpenter · Carol-Ann Davids & Micah Naidoo · Carol Laurent · Carol McKay · Carolina Pineiro · Caroline Lodge · Caroline Maldonado · Caroline Picard · Caroline Smith · Caroline Waight · Caroline West · Cassidy Hughes · Catharine Mee · Catherine Lambert · Catherine Taylor · Catriona Gibbs · Cecilia Rossi · Cecilia Uribe · Cecily Maude · Ceri Webb · Charles Fernyhough · Charles Dee Mitchell · Charles Wolfe · Charlotte Briggs · Charlotte Holtam · Charlotte Murrie & Stephen Charles · Charlotte Ryland · Charlotte Whittle · Chia Foon Yeow · China Miéville · Chris Gribble · Chris Holmes · Chris Hughes · Chris Lintott · Chris McCann · Chris Nielsen · Chris & Kathleen Repper-Day · Chris Stevenson · Christina Harris · Christine Bartels · Christine Hudnall · Christine Luker · Christopher Allen · Christopher Terry · Ciara Ní Riain · Claire Ashman · Claire Malcolm · Claire Riley · Claire Tristram · Claire Williams · Clare Archibald · Clarice Borges · Claudia Hoare · Claudia Nannini · Clifford Posner · Clive Bellingham · Clive Hewat · Colin Matthews · Colin Prendergast · Corey Nelson · Courtney Lilly · Daniel Arnold · Daniel Coxon · Daniel Douglas · Daniel Gallimore · Daniel Gillespie · Daniel Hahn · Daniel Manning · Daniel Reid · Daniel Stewart · Daniel Sweeney · Daniel Syrovy · Daniel Venn · Daniela Steierberg · Darcy Hurford · Dave Lander · Dave Young · Davi Rocha · David Anderson · David Gavin · David Hebblethwaite · David Higgins · David Johnson-Davies · David F Long · David Mantero · David Miller · David Shriver · David Smith · David Steege · David Travis · Dean Taucher · Debbie Pinfold · Declan O'Driscoll · Deirdre Nic Mhathuna · Delaina Haslam · Denis Larose · Denis Stillewagt & Anca Fronescu · Dominick Santa Cattarina · Dominique Brocard · Duncan Clubb · Duncan Marks · E Rodgers · Ed Owles · Ekaterina Beliakova · Elaine Rassaby · Eleanor Dawson · Eleanor Maier · Elhum Shakerifar · Elie Howe · Elina Zicmane · Elisabeth Cook · Eliza O'Toole · Elizabeth Cochrane · Elizabeth Draper · Elizabeth Farnsworth · Ellen Coopersmith · Ellen Kennedy · Ellen Wilkinson · Ellie Goddard · Emily Chia & Marc Ronnie · Emily Taylor · Emily Williams · Emily Yaewon Lee & Gregory Limpens · Emma Barraclough · Emma Bielecki · Emma Louise Grove · Emma Perry · Emma Reynolds · Emma Strong · Emma Teale · Emma Turesson · Emma Yearwood · Erin Braybrook · Erin Louttit · Ewan Tant · Fatima Kried · Fawzia Kane · Filiz Emre-Cooke · Finbarr Farragher · Finlay McEwan · Fiona Malby · Fiona Quinn · Florence Reynolds · Florian Duijsens · Fran Sanderson · Francesca Brooks · Francesca Fanucci · Francisco Vilhena · Frank van Orsouw · Friederike Knabe · Gabriela Lucia Garza de Linde · Gabrielle Crockatt · Gary Gorton · Gavin Collins · Gavin Smith · Gawain Espley · Geoff Copps · Geoff Fisher ·

Geoff Thrower · Geoffrey Cohen · Geoffrey Urland · George Christie · George Hawthorne · George McCaig · George Stanbury · George Wilkinson · Georgia Panteli · Geraldine Brodie · Gill Boag-Munroe · Gillian Bohnet · Gillian Grant · Gillian Spencer · Glen Bornais · Gordon Cameron · Graham R Foster · Grant Hartwell · Grant Rintoul · Guy Haslam · Gwyn Lewis · Hadil Balzan · Hank Pryor · Hannah Mayblin · Hannah Richter · Hannah Stevens · Hans Krensler · Hans Lazda · Harmony Chan · Harriet Mossop · Heather Tipon · Helen Asquith · Helen Bowell · Helen Brady · Helen Gough · Helen Swain · Helen White · Henrike Laehnemann · Henry Patino · Hilary McGrath · HL Turner-Heffer · Holly Pester · Howard Robinson · Hugh Gilmore · Iain Munro · Ian Barnett · Ian Docherty · Ian McMillan · Ian Mond · Ian Randall · Ieva Panavaite & Mariusz Hubski · Ingrid Olsen · Irene Mansfield · Irina Tzanova · Isabella Livorni · Isabella Weibrecht · Isobel Dixon · J Collins · Jacinta Perez Gavilan Torres · Jack Brown · Jackie Sullivan · Jacqueline Haskell · Jacqueline Lademann · Jacqueline Ting Lin · Jacqueline Vint · James Attlee · James Beck · James Couling · James Crossley · James Cubbon · James Lesniak · James Portlock · James Scudamore · James Tierney · James Ward · Jamie Mollart · Jamie Osborn · Jamie Walsh · Jane Mark-Lawson · Jane Roberts · Jane Woollard · Janette Ryan · Janne Støen · Jasmine Gideon · Jason Shaver · JC Sutcliffe · Jean-Jacques Regouffre · Jeff Collins · Jeffrey Davies · Jenifer Logie · Jennifer Arnold · Jennifer Bernstein · Jennifer Harvey · Jennifer Higgins · Jennifer Humbert · Jennifer O'Brien · Jennifer Petersen · Jenny Booth · Jenny Huth · Jenny Newton · Jenny Nicholls · Jeremy Koenig · Jess Howard-Armitage · Jesse Coleman · Jessica Billington · Jessica Kibler · Jethro Soutar · Jill Twist · Jim Boucherat · Jo Goodall · Jo Harding · Jo Lateu · Joan O'Malley · Joanna Flower · Joanna Luloff · Joao Pedro Bragatti Winckler · JoDee Brandon · Jodie Adams · Johan Forsell · Johan Trouw · Johanna Anderson · Johanna Eliasson · Johannes Menzel · Johannes Georg Zipp · John Berube · John Conway · John Coyne · John Down · John Gent · John Hodgson · John Kelly · John McGill · John McKee · John Royley · John Shaw · John Steigerwald · John Winkelman · Jon Riches · Jon Talbot · Jonathan Blaney · Jonathan Huston · Jonathan Jackson · Jonathan Kiehlmann · Jonathan Ruppin · Jonathan Watkiss · Jorge Cino · Joseph Cooney · Joseph Huennekens · Joseph Schreiber · Joshua Davis · Joshua McNamara · Judith Martens · Julia Hays · Julia Rochester · Julia Sutton-Mattocks · Julian Duplain · Julian Lomas · Juliana Giraldo · Julie Gibson · Juliet Swann · JW Mersky · Kaarina Hollo · Kapka Kassabova · Karen Faarbaek de Andrade Lima · Karen Jones · Karen Waloschek · Kasim Husain · Kasper Haakansson · Kasper Hartmann · Kate Attwooll · Kate Gardner · Kate Griffin · Kate McLarnon · Katharina Becker · Katharina Liehr · Katharine Freeman · Katharine Robbins · Katherine El-Salahi · Katherine Mackinnon · Katherine Skala · Katherine Sotejeff-Wilson · Kathryn Edwards · Kathryn Kasimor · Kathryn Williams · Katie Brown · Katrina Thomas · Katya Zotova · Kay Warbrick · Keith Walker · Kent McKernan · Kevin Porter · Khairunnisa Ibrahim · Kieron James · Kim Gormley · Kirsten Major · Kirsty Doole · KL Ee · Klara Rešetič · Kristin Djuve · Krystine Phelps · Lana Selby · Lander Hawes · Laura Batatota · Laura Brown · Laura Lea · Lauren Ellemore · Lauren Hyett · Laurence Laluyaux · Laurie Sheck & Jim Peck · Leah Cooper · Leeanne Parker · Leon Frey · Leonie Schwab · Leonie Smith · Lesley Lawn · Lesley Watters · Leslie Wines · Liam Buell · Liam Fleming · Liliana Lobato · Lily Levinson · Lindsay Brammer · Lindsey Stuart · Lindy van Rooyen · Lisa Edelbacher · Lisa Taylor · Liz Ketch · Liz Wilding · Lizzie Broadbent · Lizzie Coulter · Lochlan Bloom · Loretta Platts · Lori Frecker · Lorna Bleach · Lorraine Bachand · Lorraine Bramwell · Lottie Smith · Louis Roberts · Louise Musson · Louise Piper · Louise Thompson · Luc Daley · Luc Verstraete · Lucia Rotheray · Lucy Hariades · Lucy Moffatt · Lucy Summers · Lucy Wheeler · Luke Healey · Luke Williamson · Lynn Martin · M Manfre · Maeve Lambe · Maggie Humm · Maggie Livesey · Maggie Redway · Mahan L Ellison & K Ashley Dickson · Mairi Contos · Margaret Briggs · Margaret Jull Costa · Marie Bagley · Marie Cloutier · Marie Donnelly · Marina Castledine · Marina Jones · Mario Sifuentez · Mark Dawson · Mark Langston · Mark Sargent · Mark & Sarah Sheets · Mark Sztyber · Mark Waters · Marlene Adkins · Martha Gifford · Martha Nicholson · Martha Stevns · Martin Boddy · Martin Price · Martin Vosyka · Martin Whelton · Mary Carozza · Mary Ellen Nagle · Mary Wang · Marzieh Youssefi · Matt & Owen Davies · Matt Klein · Matt Sosnow · Matthew Armstrong · Matthew Banash · Matthew Black · Matthew Francis · Matthew Hamblin · Matthew Lowe · Matthew Smith · Matthew Thomas · Matthew Warshauer · Matthew Woodman · Matty Ross · Maureen Pritchard · Max Cairnduff · Max Garrone · Max Longman · Maxim

Grigoriev · Meaghan Delahunt · Megan Wittling · Melissa Beck · Melissa Danny · Melissa Quignon-Finch · Meredith Jones · Merima Jahic · Meryl Wingfield · Michael Aguilar · Michael Andal · Michael Bichko · Michael James Eastwood · Michael Gavin · Michael Johnston · Michael Moran · Michael Ward · Michelle Lotherington · Michelle Roberts · Mike Bittner · Mike Timms · Milo Waterfield · Miriam McBride · Mitchell Albert · Molly Foster · Monica Anderson · Monika Olsen · Morag Campbell · Morgan Lyons · MP Boardman · Myles Nolan · N Tsolak · Namita Chakrabarty · Nancy Foley · Nancy Oakes · Naomi Kruger · Natalie Smith · Natalie Steer · Natasha Wightman · Nathalie Atkinson · Nathan Dorr · Navi Sahota · Ned Vaught · Neil Pretty · Nicholas Brown · Nick Chapman · Nick Flegel · Nick James · Nick Nelson & Rachel Eley · Nick Rombes · Nick Sidwell · Nicola Hart · Nicola Mira · Nicola Sandiford · Nicole Matteini · Nigel Palmer · Nikki Brice · Nikolaj Ramsdal Nielsen · Nina Alexandersen · Nina de la Mer · Nina Moore · Nina Power · Noah Levin · Noelle Harrison · Olga Zilberbourg · Oliver Keens · Olivia Payne · Pam Madigan · Pamela Ritchie · Pashmina Murthy · Pat Bevins · Patricia Appleyard · Patrick McGuinness · Paul Bailey · Paul Cray · Paul Daw · Paul Griffiths · Paul Howe & Ally Hewitt · Paul Jones · Paul Munday · Paul Myatt · Paul Segal · Paula Edwards · Paula Ely · Penelope Hewett Brown · Pete Stephens · Peter McBain · Peter McCambridge · Peter Rowland · Peter Vilbig · Peter Vos · Peter Wells · Philip Carter · Philip Nulty · Philip Warren · Philipp Jarke · Philippa Wentzel · Piet Van Bockstal · PM Goodman · Portia Msimang · PRAH Foundation · Rachael Williams · Rachel Andrews · Rachel Barnes · Rachel Carter · Rachel Lasserson · Rachel Van Riel · Rachel Wadham · Rachel Watkins · Rachel Wysoker · Rachele Huennekens · Raeanne Lambert · Ralph Cowling · Rea Cris · Rebecca Braun · Rebecca Carter · Rebecca Moss · Rebecca Rosenthal · Rebekah Hughes · Réjane Collard-Walker · Rhiannon Armstrong · Richard Ashcroft · Richard Bauer · Richard Dew · Richard Gwyn · Richard Mansell · Richard McClelland · Richard Priest · Richard Shea · Richard Soundy · Rishi Dastidar · Rita Hynes · Robert Gillett · Robert Hugh-Jones · Roberta Allport · Robin Taylor · Roger Salloch · Rory Williamson · Rosanna Foster · Rose Crichton · Rosemary Rodwell · Rosie Pinhorn · Rowena McWilliams · Roxanne O'Del Ablett · Royston Tester · Roz Simpson · Rozzi Hufton · Rune Salvesen · Rupert Ziziros · S Wight · Sabine Griffiths · Sabrina Uswak · Sally Baker · Sally Dowell · Sally Foreman · Sam Gordon · Sam Reese · Sam Ruddock · Sam Stern · Samantha Sawers · Samantha Smith · Samuel Daly · Sandra Mayer · Sara Di Girolamo · Sarah Arboleda · Sarah Benson · Sarah Harwood · Sarah Jacobs · Sarah Lucas · Sarah Pybus · Sarah Watkins · Sarah Wollner · Scott Thorough · Sean Birnie · Sean Kelly · Sean Malone · Sean McGivern · Sean Stewart · Sez Kiss · Shannon Beckner · Shannon Knapp · Shaun Whiteside · Shauna Gilligan · Sheridan Marshall · Sherman Alexie · Shira Lob · Shirley Harwood · Sian O'Neill · Sian Rowe · Silvia Kwon · Simon Armstrong · Simon Clark · Simon Robertson · Simone O'Donovan · Sindre Bjugn · Siriol Hugh-Jones · SJ Bradley · SK Grout · Sofia Mostaghimi · Sonia McLintock · Sonia Pelletreau · Sophia Wickham · Soren Murhart · Srikanth Reddy · ST Dabbagh · Stacy Rodgers · Stefanie May IV · Stefano Mula · Steph Morris · Stephan Eggum · Stephanie Lacava · Stephen Eisenhammer · Stephen Pearsall · Steve Ford · Steven & Gitte Evans · Stu Sherman · Stuart Wilkinson · Subhasree Basu · Susan Higson · Susan Irvine · Susan Manser · Susanna Fidoe · Susie Roberson · Suzanne Fortey · Suzanne Lee · Swannee Welsh · Sylvie Zannier-Betts · Tamara Larsen · Tammy Watchorn · Tania Hershman · Tanja Heller · Ted Burness · Teresa Griffiths · Teresa Werner · Terry Kurgan · Terry Woodward · The Mighty Douche Softball Team · The Rookery In the Bookery · Thees Spreckelsen · Therese Oulton · Thomas Baker · Thomas Bell · Thomas Chadwick · Thomas Fritz · Thomas Mitchell · Thomas O'Rourke · Thomas van den Bout · Tiffany Lehr · Tim Theroux · Tim & Pavlina Morgan · Tina Andrews · Tina Rotherham-Winqvist · TJ Clark · Tom Darby · Tom Dixon · Tom Franklin · Tom Gray · Tom Whatmore · Tom Wilbey · Tony Bastow · Tony Messenger · Torna Russell-Hills · Tory Jeffay · Tracy Heuring · Tracy Northup · Tracy Shapley · Tracy Washington · Trevor Lewis · Trevor Wald · Val Challen · Valerie Hamra · Vanessa Dodd · Vanessa Nolan · Veronica Barnsley · Victor Meadowcroft · Victoria Adams · Victoria Maitland · Victoria Seaman · Victoria Smith · Vijay Pattisapu · Vikki O'Neill · Vilis Kasims · Virginia Weir · Visaly Muthusamy · Wendy Langridge · Wendy Olson · Wendy Peate · Will Huxter · William Brockenborough · William Dennehy · William Mackenzie · William Schwartz · Zoë Brasier

ALICIA KOPF is a writer and artist based in Barcelona. *Brother in Ice* is the culmination of an artistic cycle of exhibitions entitled *Àrticantàrtic*. The original Catalan manuscript of *Brother in Ice* won the 2015 Premi Documenta, a prestigious prize for an unpublished Catalan-language work of literature, and upon publication was awarded the 2016 Premi Llibreter by Catalan booksellers. The Spanish edition received further prizes, including the Premio El Ojo Crítico, awarded by Spanish National Radio.

MARA FAYE LETHEM is based between Barcelona and Brooklyn, and translates from Catalan and Spanish. She has translated many contemporary novelists, and is a reviewer for the *New York Times*.